Masks don't fool masked men

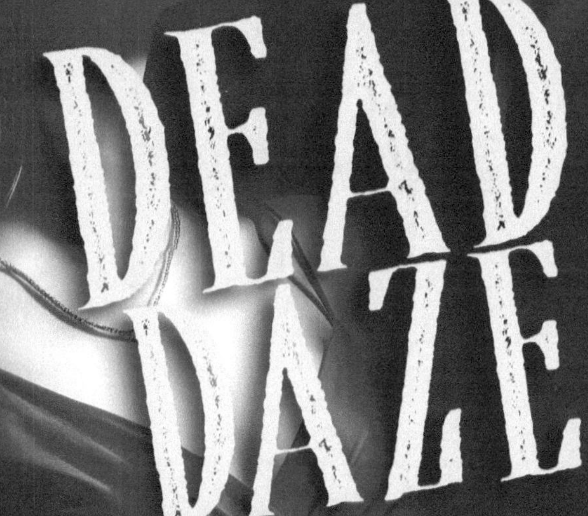

DEAD DAZE
new york times bestselling author
ja huss

DEAD DAZE
Copyright © 2026 by JA Huss
Cover design by JA Huss
ISBN: 978-1-957277-58-5
All rights reserved.

ABOUT THE BOOK

ABOUT THE BOOK

6 Months. No Answers. No Closure. No Contact.

ScarletSins

Check here if you've moved on. I have a new apartment.

Check here if you've forgotten him. I write in coffee shops now.

This is my life. Normal. Safe. Boring. I date men who don't know my real name. I drink lattes and pretend I'm someone who drinks lattes.

Why am I doing this?

Because the alternative is admitting I'm still his.

Six months. No answers. No closure. No contact.

I'm fine.

Watcher

Check here if you've given her space. I follow from three cars back.

Check here if you've stopped watching. I've memorized her new coffee order.

This is my restraint. No cameras. No contact. No crossing

the lines she drew. I watch her pretend to write. Pretend to date. Pretend to be someone who forgot me.

Why am I doing this?

Because she asked me to leave her alone.

Then she laughed at his joke.

And I remembered—I never agreed to let her go.

Some monsters know how to wait. Others just learn when to stop.

VIBES

🖤💔🔥 Second Chance Romance

🏃🦴👁 She Ran/He Followed

🔥👁🦴 Jealous MMC

👁🔪🖤 Stalker Hero

📓🦴💀 He Never Let Go

🔪🖤🔥 Obsessive Hero

👀📚🌶 He Reads Her Books

😈🦴🖤 She's Mine

💀⚔🔥 Touch Her and Find Out

🖤🧎💀 Pitch Black MMC

🐺🏃🔥 Predator/Prey

💰🦴💼 Claimed by a Billionaire

🏃🌀🦴 The Chase

🎂🔥🖤 Age Gap

💼🦴🖤 Power Imbalance

▶💀🖤 Did I Mention Pitch Black?

CHAPTER 1
SCARLETTA

I'm half-awake when the words come.

They always come like this—slipping in through the cracks in my consciousness before I'm fully present, before I can judge them or shut them down.

Ivy stands outside the sleek black door of Velvet Underground, clutching the embossed invitation Logan slipped under her apartment door three days ago. Her hands shake. Inside, masked strangers are doing things nice girls don't think about. Things she's been thinking about for months.

"You won't actually go," Logan told her last week. He was leaning against the doorframe of her apartment with that infuriating smirk. "You'll fantasize about it. Write about it in that little journal you think I don't know about. But you won't walk through my door."

She hates that he's right.

She hates that her pussy is already wet just standing here.

My hand slides between my thighs on autopilot, fingers finding the familiar path. I press against my clit, trying to chase the heat. Trying to follow Ivy into Logan's club where masked attendants will strip her bare and—

Nothing.

I'm not even wet.

I keep trying anyway, circling my clit, waiting for my body to catch up to the story playing in my head. Ivy's embarrassment, her shame, her desperate need for Logan to see her—

Nothing.

I pull my hand away and stare at the ceiling of my new apartment.

Six months.

It's been six months since Story Island. Six months since I destroyed every camera. Six months since I've heard Caleb's voice.

Six months since I've been able to come.

I throw off the covers and get out of bed because what's the fucking point of lying here pretending?

The master bathroom gleams with imported Portuguese tiles—soft blues and whites arranged in geometric patterns that conjure up images of Saint Lawrence. The walk-in closet attached to it is mostly empty except for the few things I bought when I moved in, but I like what it represents. Space I could fill if I wanted to.

After I pee, I wander back out into the living room, my bare feet silent on the hardwood.

This apartment is four times the size of my old place. Twenty-five hundred dollars a month—that's what this much space costs in downtown Idaho Falls.

The walls are painted a sophisticated sage green with tan and ecru accent colors highlighting the baseboards and crown molding. The floors are dark walnut hardwood, polished to a subtle sheen, and the floor-to-ceiling windows are framed in six-inch wood boards stained to match.

Like an actual interior designer sat down and made deliberate choices instead of just slapping beige paint over everything and calling it done.

The building itself is gorgeous. A four-story brick walkup

from the 1920s that used to be the town's central bank. Only four units total—one per floor. I'm on the third. My balcony is big enough for a full patio set, though I haven't bought one. Two bedrooms, two baths, and it came completely furnished with butter-soft leather couches in that same ecru tone and a dining table I've never used.

The whole place really is beautiful in a way that still makes me uncomfortable—like I'm house-sitting for someone who actually belongs here.

I drift toward the far window, the one facing south, and pull back the heavy curtain. Natural light spills across the hardwood, warm and golden even though it's barely past dawn. Beyond the glass, the view opens up—the Snake River Greenbelt unfurling like a ribbon of green through the downtown corridor, the water itself visible in slivers between tree branches. Early morning mist still clings to the surface, and I can just make out the shape of a jogger moving along the paved trail.

I stand there for a long moment, my forehead nearly touching the cool glass, watching the jogger disappear around the bend where the trail curves toward the Japanese Friendship Garden. The light shifts as the sun climbs higher, burning through the last of the mist, turning the river from pewter to something almost silver.

They say that a view like this can save you. That if you just look at something beautiful enough, peaceful enough, long enough—if you let the green and the water and the wide-open sky do their work—eventually the noise in your head will quiet down. Eventually you'll feel something other than the dull, persistent ache of going through the motions.

I'm counting on it.

Because I've tried everything else.

I turn away from the window, leaving the river view behind, and make my way back through the bedroom to the walk-in closet. I haven't accumulated much in the months I've been here, haven't felt the urge to fill it with things that might anchor me to this place more permanently than I'm ready for.

I pull on a pair of black running shorts with the kind of moisture-wicking fabric I never used to care about, then reach for the matching sports bra hanging on the hook beside them. The tank top is a muted shade of grey-blue that reminds me of storm clouds.

I sit on the edge of the bed to lace up my running shoes. They're the kind serious runners wear, the kind I researched obsessively before buying, reading reviews and comparing cushioning technology like it mattered.

Like any of this matters.

When they're tied, I head to the kitchen and grab a bottle of water from the fridge, sliding it into the back pocket of my running vest. The vest itself is a relatively new addition to my collection of things I never thought I'd own—lightweight mesh, reflective strips, multiple pockets for phone, and keys, and energy gels I don't actually use.

I slip my phone into the front pocket, feeling the familiar weight of it settle against my ribs.

Six months ago, I didn't even know what a running vest was. I certainly didn't need one—it's not like I'm out here making TikToks about "The Running Effect" or documenting my fitness journey for an audience of strangers, though I do record my runs on the app just for the sake of having something to show for the hours I spend on the Greenbelt.

The data, the metrics, the proof that I moved my body through space, and burned calories, and logged miles. I just felt left out, I guess. Like the new girl on the Snake River trail, watching all the serious runners go by with their gear, and their purpose, and their easy confidence.

I hate that I bought this shit. The vest, the shoes, the expensive athletic wear that makes me look like I belong in this version of my life.

I love that I have it. That I can put the vest on and become someone who runs, someone who fits in, someone who looks like they have their shit together.

Life shouldn't be this contradictory.

Why is it always so confusing?

I descend the stairs and step out into the late August morning, breathing in the crisp air that still carries a hint of coolness before the day heats up. The sun is just beginning its climb over the eastern horizon, painting the sky in soft shades of pink and orange that fade into pale blue. The streets are quiet—most of the downtown shops won't open for hours yet, and the serious morning runners have already completed their first loops.

I walk the couple of blocks to the river at an easy pace, rolling my shoulders, shaking out my arms, letting my muscles gradually wake up. It's something I learned the hard way during those first brutal weeks after I moved here—how you can't just throw your body into motion without warning, how tendons protest and joints lock up if you don't ease them into it first. How much it hurts when you're too impatient, too desperate to outrun whatever's chasing you through your own head.

Then, once I reach the Greenbelt, once my feet hit the familiar paved trail that runs alongside the Snake River, I start to jog. Not fast. Never fast. Just a steady, sustainable pace that lets my mind drift while my body moves on autopilot.

And I let the words come.

The story.

Third person now, not first.

Ivy and Logan.

Logan opens the heavy door of Velvet Underground, his hand firm on the small of Ivy's back as he guides her through. The lighting inside is dim—ambient reds and purples that cast everyone in soft shadows. There are people everywhere. On couches, on platforms, against walls. Some are dressed in leather and latex, others are completely naked.

Ivy's breath catches when she realizes what's happening on the central stage—a woman bent over a padded bench while a man fucks her from behind, slow and deliberate, his hands gripping her hips. The woman's face is visible in profile, and she's not faking. Her mouth is open, eyes squeezed shut, and when she moans it echoes through the club.

"Everyone's watching," Logan murmurs against Ivy's ear. "Everyone can see how hard she's taking it. How much she loves it."

Ivy's pussy clenches involuntarily.

Logan leads her to a private alcove separated from the main floor by sheer black curtains. Not truly private—anyone can see through if they look—but removed enough to feel like a secret. There's a leather couch, a low table with bottles of water and condoms, and mirrors on two walls.

"Strip," Logan says. Not harsh. Just certain.

Ivy's hands shake as she pulls her dress over her head. She's wearing the black lace lingerie he told her to buy and his eyes darken when he sees it.

"Fuck," he breathes. "You did exactly what I told you."

He's on her before she can respond, his mouth claiming hers, his hands everywhere. He unhooks her bra with practiced ease, cups her breasts, thumbs her nipples until she's gasping against his mouth. When he slides his hand into her panties, his fingers find her dripping wet.

"Christ, Ivy. You're soaked." He pushes two fingers inside her without warning, and she moans so loudly someone beyond the curtain laughs.

"They can hear you," Logan tells her, pumping his fingers slowly. "They know what we're doing. They're watching through the curtain, imagining your tight little pussy stretched around my fingers."

Ivy should be mortified. She should pull away, tell him this is too much, she can't—

But her hips are grinding against his hand, chasing the pressure, desperate for more.

I stop running.

My chest heaves, my pulse thundering in my ears, and I press my hands against my knees, trying to catch my breath.

The fantasy isn't working.

It should be working. Ivy's exactly the kind of protagonist I've always loved writing—awkward, ashamed, desperate to surrender to someone who sees through her performance. Logan's the perfect dominant—confident, controlling, obsessed with breaking down her walls.

The sex club scene is hot. I know it's hot. I can feel the architecture of the arousal, the way the layers should stack— public humiliation, forced confession, the terror of being watched mixing with the desperate need to be seen.

I understand the mechanics.

My pussy doesn't care.

I straighten up and look around. I'm about three miles into the Greenbelt now, near the section where the trail curves away from the river and into a thicker stretch of trees. There's a cluster of large boulders just off the path, partially hidden by scrub brush and cottonwood saplings.

Semi-private.

I could duck behind them. Pull my shorts to the side. Try to finish what Ivy and Logan started.

The thought sends absolutely nothing through my body.

No heat. No clench. No wetness spreading between my thighs.

Just the same dull, empty ache that's been living inside me for six months.

I close my eyes and let myself imagine it—just for a second. Just to see if maybe…

It comes to me immediately.

The memory, the scene, the arousal…

Caleb standing over a motionless heap of dead flesh, his

fist working up and down the length of his massive, hard cock with brutal, punishing strokes. His jaw is locked tight and his eyes are fixed on the corpse at his feet—watching his come explode in thick, obscene ropes across the still-warm body of the Russian intruder he just beat to death.

The visual is so visceral I can hear the wet sound of his sticky hand slapping against his flesh, can see the tendons standing out in his forearm as he grips himself harder.

His breathing comes in controlled, measured pants, not from exertion but from something darker, more primal.

His face is a mask of cold satisfaction—not pleasure exactly, but the fulfilled look of a man who's taken exactly what he wanted, consequences be damned.

I can practically smell the blood. Almost see the way his come glistens against the body at his feet.

His gaze is so intense, like he's memorizing every detail. Cataloging the exact way his seed marks his victory.

There's no remorse in his expression, no horror at what he's done—only a terrible, perfect focus.

My clit pulses.

Once.

Sharp and undeniable.

"Fuck," I whisper.

No.

Absolutely not.

I'm not doing this. I'm not indulging the fantasy of the man who came over a dead, bloody body.

I'm not getting wet thinking about Caleb MacLeay.

I won't.

I start running again, harder this time, pushing my pace until my lungs burn, and my thighs scream, and there's no room left in my head for anything except the physical demand of keeping my body moving forward.

No Ivy.

No Logan.

No sex club.

No masked man with his cock inside my pussy, whispering into my ear, telling me I'm exactly the kind of broken he needs.

Just the rhythm of my feet hitting pavement.

Just the river beside me, indifferent and cold.

Just the empty, hollow space where my desire used to live.

Back at the apartment, I strip off my running clothes and step into the shower, turning the water hot enough to scald. The steam fills the bathroom until I can barely see my own hand pressed against the tile.

I scrub hard. Wash my hair. Shave my legs even though there's no one to feel them.

When I finally step out, I dress in the first thing I grab from the drawer—denim shorts and a black tank top. Nothing special. Nothing that requires thought.

I zip my new laptop into my backpack, slinging it over one shoulder. Purchased because my old laptop is still sitting in the blanket fort in my old apartment.

The apartment I haven't moved out of.

The apartment I still pay rent on every month—on time now, with money left over.

The irony isn't lost on me. Eight months ago, I was four months behind on a studio I could barely afford. Now I'm paying for two places.

The old one because I can't bring myself to pack up the wreckage, and this new one because living in the squalor of your own depression doesn't heal you, and I desperately want to be healed.

Fixed.

Normal.

I grab my keys and leave.

The coffee shop is three blocks away, tucked into the ground floor of another converted historic building. I order a latte—whole milk, extra shot—and find my usual corner table by the window.

I pull out the laptop, open it, and stare at the blank document on the screen.

Cursor blinking.

Waiting.

I type: *Ivy pressed her back against the wall as Logan—*

Delete.

The curtains at Velvet Underground were—

Delete.

I close the document without saving and open a browser instead, scrolling aimlessly through social media I don't post to, articles I don't finish reading, anything that looks like productivity from a distance.

People come and go around me. I watch them all. I pretend to work.

I haven't written a single fucking word since I got home from Story Island.

When the tables start filling up around noon, I pack up my laptop, leave, and walk home.

Third outfit change. Athletic leggings, sports bra, oversized tee knotted at my hip.

Grab a second backpack already pre-loaded with gear. Shove a beef stick into my mouth, eat a second one on the drive. Guzzle some water.

The gym is six blocks away, but closer to the river. I've been coming every day since I moved in to the new apartment. The front desk staff know my name. The regulars nod when I walk past the free weights.

I smile back. Wave sometimes. Ask how their weekend was.

I'm outgoing here. Friendly, even.

I'm performing *normal girl who goes to the gym.*

None of them know I'm just killing time.

I claim a treadmill, plug in my earbuds, and run. Again. Miles I don't need, burning energy I don't have. When my legs start shaking, I switch to the stair climber and punish myself for another thirty minutes.

I'm not training for anything.

I'm not working toward a goal.

I'm just… here.

I shower. Fourth outfit change. Strappy-back jumpsuit in lavender made of organic cotton because that kind of shit matters in the next place.

Today's yoga studio is across town.

This is where I meet men.

Soy boy feminists who've never seen a pair of handcuffs outside a joke shop. Men who say things like "I really respect your boundaries" and "consent is so important to me" with the earnest intensity of someone who's never had a dark thought in their entire life.

I've been on twelve dates since Caleb.

Twelve different men from twelve different yoga classes scattered across many different studios. Each studio has dozens of classes. I almost never run into the same guy twice unless I want to.

I don't want to.

One date, maybe two if he's boring enough to be safe.

Never a third.

Today's class is at 4 PM in a studio I've only been to twice before. I recognize no one, which is perfect. I unroll my mat in the back corner and sink into child's pose while the instructor dims the lights and starts the playlist—something with chimes and a woman's voice humming.

I'm surprisingly flexible these days.

All that running. All that gym time. All those hours spent anywhere but in my own head.

I flow through the poses on autopilot. Downward dog. Warrior two. Triangle. My body bends and stretches and holds, and I feel absolutely nothing.

After class, I eat a take-out salad in my car, then drive to the community center on the east side.

Not to a "I'm a sick submissive who gets off on men coming on dead bodies" support group, because those don't exist.

To a divorced women's support group.

They don't check ID at the door, and no one asks follow-up questions when you say you're "going through something" so I sit in the circle of folding chairs and listen to the stories.

Margaret's ex-husband emptied their bank accounts and moved to Florida with his dental hygienist.

Sharon's fighting for custody of her kids even though she supports the family and her ex hasn't worked a job since he made sandwiches in college.

Linda just wants to know if it's normal to cry every time she sees a couple holding hands at the grocery store.

I like the stories.

I'm ashamed of this.

I'm ashamed that I sit here, pretending to belong, harvesting other people's pain like research notes for a book I'll never write.

But I come back anyway.

I have a whole list of them set up all across the city. This and the yoga was the whole reason I bought myself a new Jeep. Black, lifted, aggressive muddy tires the size of small planets. Something that screams "I belong here, I'm one of you, I've always been local"—which is technically true, but also the most pathetic kind of lie. Because I don't leave town. I don't venture into the Tetons for hikes or climbs.

I hoard support groups like they're gold and yoga classes like they might save me.

I've attended every 'Anonymous' group within twenty miles over the past six months. Depression groups. Illness support circles. Grief counseling. Addiction recovery. Trauma survivors. I don't discriminate.

If it eats hours in my day, I'm in.

When the session ends, I slip out before anyone can ask how I'm doing.

Home again. Third shower of the day.

I stand under the spray until the water runs cold, then wrap myself in a towel and crawl into bed.

I pull up the Ivy and Logan scene from my head… maybe tonight it'll work.

Maybe tonight my body will remember how to want something.

I slide my hand between my thighs.

Nothing.

I try anyway. Force myself to focus on the scene—Logan's fingers inside Ivy, the strangers watching through the curtain, the humiliation and desire tangled together.

I give up after five minutes and blank my mind.

This is my life now.

Coffee shops, and gyms, and yoga classes, and support groups I don't belong to.

Running from nothing. Toward nothing.

Pretending I'm fine.

Pretending I'm normal.

Pretending I don't spend every night trying to masturbate to fantasies that don't work anymore because the only thing that gets me wet is the memory of a man ejaculating on a corpse.

I turn off the light.

I turn off my life.

I turn off everything.

Because if I don't turn it off then I'll have to admit that what Caleb did...

How he did it...

How he *looked*—his eyes, his jaw, his grip on his cock, the way his come spewed out in streams...

Was... *hot*.

CHAPTER 2
CALEB

Snow fills my vision. Her footprints, already disappearing under fresh powder. The shape of her body in the drift where I tackled her.

I stand naked at my bedroom window, forehead pressed against the cold glass, looking out at the summer forest of lodgepole pines and quaking aspen.

I'm focused on the exact spot where she screamed.

Help! Someone help me!

The forest doesn't look anything like it did that morning. The snow has been gone so long now, it's about to come back. The leaves of the aspen grove are already starting to yellow and the elderberry bushes are heavy with clusters of nearly-black berries.

Time.

It passes whether you want it to or not.

That morning last Christmas I chased her naked through the snow. Watched her stumble and fall and get up and run again, her bare feet red from the freezing cold.

My cock was hard the entire time. It had every right to be. What we were doing—her running, me chasing—this made sense. I'd been fucking her like a monster for eight straight hours.

Of course, I was hard.

Scarletta herself had written these chase scenes. Dozens of times. It's arousing. The chase, the capture, the surrender. A common fantasy. Perfectly normal.

Except…

I pace away from the window, then back.

Except when I looked down at her as I pinned her in the snow and she looked back at me—really saw me—there was nothing in her eyes but fear.

Not the fear she writes about. Not the fear that bleeds into arousal, that transforms into trust.

Just fear.

Raw. Animal. Survival.

The kind that says *this man will kill me.*

I stuck a needle in her thigh anyway.

I told myself it was necessary. She was hypothermic, irrational, putting herself in danger. I was protecting her from herself.

I was so fucking sure.

Now, as I stare at the place where I held her down, I'm not sure of anything.

Turning away, I walk over to the bed and sit down on the edge. Elbows on my knees, face in my hands.

Story Island.

The maze.

Volk.

That was nothing like Christmas morning. It was supposed to be better. Less clinical, more challenging. Climbing rope ladders into trees. Bending over punishment benches sixty feet in the air. A zip-line taxi to the next station.

It was supposed to be fun.

The maze wasn't a punishment, it was her deepest,

darkest fantasy come to life. The fantasy that filled her with so much shame, she hid it away. Denying its existence.

We got to know each other better after her safe word in station 2. We came to an understanding.

At least… I thought we did.

I see it from her perspective now. What she must have seen.

Scarletta crouched in the mud, covered in blood that wasn't hers, watching a headless body leak out onto the platform where I was supposed to fuck her. She was screaming her safeword and nobody came. She thought the attendants were part of the scene. She thought I'd scripted her terror.

Then I arrived.

Naked. Erect. Already hard from watching her preparation on the monitors.

She watched me torture a man.

Cut off his fingers. His cock. His balls.

She watched me stroke myself while I did it.

My hand moves to my dick automatically. The memory shouldn't arouse me.

It absolutely does.

Volk's screams.

The way his body convulsed when I severed the femoral.

The hot spray of arterial blood across my chest.

I came on his corpse.

Scarletta saw all of it.

I told myself it was justice. I told myself Volk trafficked five hundred children and deserved worse than I gave him. I told myself she'd understand because I'd already confessed to killing Derek.

But Derek happened off-camera. Derek was a story I told her. A monster I'd already slain before she knew it existed.

Volk was different.

Volk was immediate. Visceral. Real.

I made Scarletta watch me become the thing I actually am.

Not the controlled dominant who edges her, and praises her, and makes her feel safe while she surrenders.

The other thing.

The monster who gets hard from killing.

Who comes harder from violence than from her sweet wet pussy.

My cock throbs in my hand and I hate myself for it.

But do I stop jerking on it?

Do I even attempt to control myself?

No.

Why should I?

Isn't this the whole point?

Isn't embracing my nature the entire fucking point?

I want to be who I am.

I want to kill motherfuckers who deserve it.

I want to balance the scales.

I want to watch the faces of these monsters, see that moment of terror that flashes across their eyes when they realize it's over.

Coming on them is just… what they deserve.

It's justice.

I stroke myself harder, chasing the edge.

Is it fucked up that killing gets me off?

Yes.

Obviously.

But I've built a world where it makes sense. Where the violence has purpose. Direction. Intent.

I kill men who traffic children. Men who rape. Men who destroy lives and walk away clean because they have money, connections, lawyers who know which judges to buy.

The system fails.

I don't.

So what if my cock gets hard when I pull the trigger? So

what if I come when they bleed out? At least I'm pointing this sickness at the right targets.

At least I understand that the innocent are not commodities to be bought and sold.

Women. Children. The vulnerable.

They're not products.

The auction is different.

The auction is fantasy. Controlled. Negotiated. A contract between two consenting adults who both walk away satisfied.

Is it weird?

Maybe.

But isn't everything about this world weird?

People get off on power dynamics. Surrender. Control. The illusion of danger wrapped in absolute safety.

It's an excuse to do things without guilt. To explore the darker edges of desire in a contained environment where nobody gets actually hurt.

Scarletta wanted it.

She checked the boxes herself. TPE. Forced confession. Psychological dominance. She gave me permission to weaponize her own writing against her.

She wrote the maze.

I just built it.

If she didn't want to be hunted by monsters, why did she spend forty-two thousand words describing exactly how it should feel?

The logic holds.

I stroke myself faster, chasing the edge. My other hand braces against my thigh, gripping hard enough to leave marks.

Heat floods my abdomen. My balls draw up tight. Every muscle in my core tightens, coiling.

I see Volk's face. The moment he realized. The exact second understanding hit—that I wasn't going to let him walk away. That money, and connections, and diplomatic immunity meant nothing here.

That terror.

That absolute helplessness.

My cock pulses in my hand.

I see the knife cutting through his Achilles tendons. The way his legs spasmed. The scream that tore out of him when he understood what came next.

My breathing goes ragged.

I see myself circling him. Naked. Hard. Deliberate.

He knew what I was.

He knew exactly what kind of monster stood in front of him.

And there was nothing he could do about it.

My hand moves faster, rougher. I don't bother with finesse. I'm not performing for anyone. This is just me and what I am.

I see the blood spraying across my chest. My stomach. My cock.

The way Volk's body jerked and thrashed while he bled out.

The way I kept stroking myself, matching my rhythm to his dying heartbeat.

"Fuck," I grind out. My voice sounds wrecked.

Pressure builds at the base of my spine. My thighs shake.

I see Scarletta's face. Her eyes wide. Watching me come on a corpse.

Watching me become exactly what I am.

The image pushes me over.

I bend forward, groaning as my orgasm slams through me. Come shoots across the hardwood floor in thick ropes. My cock jerks in my fist, spilling everywhere—the floor, my hand, my thigh.

I don't stop stroking. I milk every pulse, every aftershock, my whole body shuddering through it.

When it finally passes, I'm bent over, panting.

Come pools on the floor beneath me.

I don't feel ashamed.

I just breathe.

This is managed.

I know what I am. I know what arouses me.

I know the sickness lives inside me.

I understand I can't kill it.

But I can point it at the right targets.

I can make it serve justice instead of chaos.

I can control when, and where, and how it manifests.

That's the difference between me and the men I kill.

They hurt the innocent.

I don't.

So… the logic holds.

It has to hold.

Because if it doesn't—if the auction wasn't consent, if the maze wasn't her fantasy, if I'm not the controlled dominant who gives her what she needs—

Then what the fuck am I?

I stand in the kitchen of the log mansion, coffee steeping inside the French press as I stare at the three monitors mounted above the breakfast bar.

It's been six months since Scarletta got out of my limo on Valentine's Day.

Six months is plenty of time to process.

Plenty of time to recover.

The perfect distance to understand what we are.

What she needs.

The doubts from earlier are gone now. My orgasm cleared them out like smoke through an open window. My head is sharp again. Sharp and focused.

I know what I'm doing.

The coffee finishes. I press the plunger down slowly, watching the grounds sink. Pour it black into a ceramic mug and take a sip.

Perfect.

Everything is perfect today.

I look good, too. Tom Ford suit. Charcoal grey, three-piece. Fit is perfect. Silk tie in deep burgundy. Shoes are Church's, polished to a mirror shine.

All three monitors show the Idaho Falls Greenbelt trail at different locations.

I lean closer, as a figure appears on the riverwalk that follows the Snake River trail. I hold my breath, waiting to recognize—yes. It's her. Scarletta is so punctual these days. Always right on time. She's wearing black leggings and a matching fitted tank top. She's got her hair pulled back in a high ponytail that swings when she runs.

She looks healthy.

Better than healthy, she looks absolutely gorgeous.

Like someone who has her life together.

I take a sip of coffee, studying her form as she breaks into a slow jog. Posture is good. Breathing steady. She runs like she's training for something, not just passing time.

This is progress.

Real progress.

She hasn't logged into DarkDesires in six months. Not once. I check daily—her account sits dormant, followers still asking where she went, when she's coming back, if everything is okay.

Radio silence.

At first, I was concerned. Wondered if I broke something fundamental. If the maze, the blood, watching me kill Volk— if it shattered her completely.

But then I realized… she's not broken.

She's *stacking*.

Writers do this. They go dark for months, building up material, refining their craft. Then they come back with something massive. Something that redefines their entire body of work.

That's what she's doing.

She must be.

She is.

She's writing our story. The truth of what happened between us dressed up as pitch-black fiction. The auction. The cabin. Story Island. All of it.

She just hasn't shared it yet.

Not because she's ashamed.

Because it's not ready.

Because *she's* not ready.

That's all. That's why.

On the screen, Scarletta's pace has intensified. The morning light catches the sheen of sweat forming at her temples. She's pushing herself today—harder than usual.

I watch the fluidity of her stride, the controlled aggression in each footfall. This isn't the tentative jogging of someone going through motions. This is someone running *toward* something. Or away from it.

Either way, it's movement.

It's life.

It's so far removed from the girl who used to sit hunched over her laptop for sixteen hours straight, forgetting to eat, forgetting the world existed beyond her fiction.

When she's done, she'll go home, shower, put on something cute, do her hair and makeup, then walk the four blocks to Cornerstone.

She'll order a latte.

She'll sit in the corner with her laptop, watching the crowd of people ebb and flow as the hours pass.

Then she'll leave, go to the gym and continue her day like the maze never happened. Like the auction was a dream.

Spoiler alert, Scarletta. It wasn't. And it's time I helped you remembered that.

Just… a reminder.

That I'm still here.

That I still want her. Still need her.

That it's time to begin again.

I finish my coffee, rinse the mug, set it in the sink.

Today is a special day.

Today, Scarletta learns I haven't forgotten her.

That I will *never* forget her.

That she is *unforgettable*.

CHAPTER 3
SCARLETTA

The early August evening is still warm when I walk through downtown Idaho Falls toward the pizza place. My sundress is light yellow—pretty, feminine, carefully chosen to signal *available but not desperate*. The fabric swishes against my thighs with each step. I've got my hair down, curled at the ends. Makeup applied with actual effort instead of the bare minimum I usually manage.

I look normal.

Like someone who goes on dates.

Like someone who hasn't spent six months unable to come without thinking about a man murdering someone.

Marty is waiting inside Provisions Pizza when I push through the door. He waves immediately, standing up from the booth with this eager-puppy energy that should be endearing but mostly just makes me tired.

He's tall. Blond. Clean-shaven. His yoga-instructor body is obvious even under his casual button-down. We met yesterday during the post-class cool-down when he asked if I wanted to grab coffee sometime. I said yes because I'm supposed to. Because normal girls say yes when normal guys ask them out.

Because I need to prove I'm not completely ruined.

"Scarletta! Hey, you look amazing." He gestures to the booth seat across from him.

"Thanks." I slide in, setting my purse beside me. "Sorry if I'm a little late."

"No, you're perfect. Right on time, actually."

I'm starving. Like actually hungry for the first time in weeks. When the waitress comes over, I order the specialty—a pizza pie with extra cheese and pepperoni. Marty gets a salad because of course he does.

"So I was thinking after dinner, maybe we could grab drinks at that new place on the river?" He's leaning forward, hands folded on the table. Engaged. Present.

"Oh, I can't stay out late tonight." The lie comes automatically. "Early morning tomorrow."

"No problem! We can keep it casual."

I smile and nod, already knowing I won't be going anywhere after this meal. I never stay out after dark. Ever. The rule is absolute. Daylight only. Public places only. Home before the streetlights come on.

Because I'm not ready to confront what happens when the sun goes down and I'm alone with someone.

Marty starts talking about his business—some kind of paint-your-own-pottery studio in the neighborhood next to mine. A place where couples go on date nights to make ugly mugs and pretend they're being creative together.

"—and we're expanding to offer wine and painting classes on Friday nights. You know, like those viral videos where everyone gets a little tipsy and paints the same sunset?"

"Mm-hmm." I nod along, watching his mouth move.

Could I fuck this guy?

The thought appears unbidden. Clinical. I study him while he talks—his strong jawline, the definition in his forearms where he's rolled up his sleeves, the way his hands move when he gestures. He's objectively attractive. Fit. Successful enough to own his own business at twenty-two.

I try to picture it. His body over mine. His hands sliding up my thighs. His fingers pushing inside me—

Nothing.

Absolutely nothing.

My pussy doesn't respond. My pulse doesn't quicken. It's like watching paint dry while someone describes sex to me in medical terminology.

"So what do you do?" Marty asks, pulling me back.

I blink. Scramble for the prepared answer. "I'm a freelance writer. Mostly marketing copy, some blog content. Working from home."

All lies.

I haven't written a single word in six months. Haven't taken a freelance gig. Haven't earned a dollar beyond what's sitting in my bank account from—

No. Not thinking about that.

"That's cool! What kind of stuff do you write about?"

"Boring corporate things." I wave my hand dismissively. "Product descriptions. SEO optimization. Nothing exciting."

The pizza arrives and I'm grateful for the interruption. I take a massive bite, barely tasting it, just needing something to do with my mouth besides construct more elaborate fictions about who I am.

Marty keeps talking. Something about expansion plans. Something about hiring part-time staff. Something about his lease negotiations.

I nod. Smile. Laugh when his tone suggests I should.

But inside, I'm spiraling.

What if I asked him outright? *Hey Marty, do you have a freak side? Because I need someone who can make me come and apparently regular sex isn't going to cut it anymore.*

Yoga guys don't. They're too... gentle. Too balanced. Too fucking *mindful*.

They want to make love slowly while maintaining eye contact and asking if you're comfortable every thirty seconds.

I can already picture Marty naked. His cut abs. His careful hands. The way he'd probably ask permission before touching my breast. The way he'd be *so considerate* about my pleasure while completely failing to understand what I actually need.

My mind shifts unbidden.

What if I flipped the script entirely?

What if I became the dominant one? What if I made Marty bend over a bench in his stupid pottery studio, made him wait there with his cock hard and exposed while I decided whether to touch him—

The image crystallizes. Marty's perfect ass in the air. His dick hanging between his legs. Waiting for me to spank him. Waiting for me to use him.

And I feel... nothing.

Worse than nothing.

I feel repulsed.

The thought of controlling someone, of being the one in charge, of wielding power over another person's body—it makes my stomach turn. It's so fundamentally wrong that I physically recoil, closing my eyes and shaking my head to dislodge the vision.

"Hey, you okay?" Marty's voice cuts through.

I open my eyes. He's staring at me with concern, his salad fork frozen halfway to his mouth.

"Yeah, sorry. Just—" I force a laugh. "Brain fog. Low blood sugar probably."

"You should eat." He gestures to my pizza. "Seriously, take your time."

I take another bite, chewing mechanically while Marty watches me with those kind, worried eyes.

Normal girls would be charmed by this.

Normal girls would appreciate a guy who checks in, who notices when something's off.

But I'm not normal.

I haven't been normal in a very long time.

And sitting here with Marty, pretending I could ever be satisfied by someone this safe, this *vanilla*, feels like the cruelest joke I've played on myself yet.

Marty leans forward across the table, his whole posture shifting. The casual yoga instructor energy drains away. His eyes lock onto mine—not the polite, friendly gaze from before. Something sharper. More focused.

"Can I ask you a question?"

His voice is different. Deeper. The careful brightness stripped out of it.

A tiny buzz sparks low in my belly. So faint I almost miss it.

"Sure," I say, setting down my pizza slice.

He opens his mouth. Closes it. His fingers drum against the table edge—once, twice—then stop. His jaw works like he's chewing words he can't quite swallow.

I smile despite myself. "What's the problem?"

"I just—" He stops again. Looks down at his salad, then back up at me. "There are different kinds of guys, right? Like, there's the… the sensitive type. The ones who do couples yoga and talk about their feelings and want to build emotional intimacy before—before anything physical."

I nod slowly, watching him struggle.

"And then there's the… the dominant guys. The ones who take charge. Who make decisions. Who—" He clears his throat. "Who want control. But not in a toxic way. In like, a—a structured way."

The buzz intensifies. Just barely.

"And then there's—there's somewhere in the middle, I guess. Guys who adapt. Who can be whatever their partner needs." His fingers resume drumming. Stop again. "Or guys who pretend to be one thing because they think that's what women want, but they're actually—"

He cuts himself off, breathing harder.

I wait.

"What's your type?" he finally asks.

The question hangs between us.

I tilt my head. "Are you asking if *you're* my type?"

Marty shrugs. "Well, I'm not sure if that's what I'm asking. Actually, no. That's not what I'm asking because you don't know me, so how could you possibly know I'm your type?"

I let out a breath and lean back in the booth. OK. I guess this guy wants to have some real talk. Unexpected, but not entirely unwanted. "So… what *are* you asking?"

"Well…" he looks me straight in the eyes. I'm talking, locked the fuck on. "I'm asking which one you prefer. Do you like soft guys?"

"Like you?"

He laughs. "Am I soft?"

I shrug. "You look a little soft."

"Why? Because I take yoga?"

"Yes. Mostly. But also… I dunno. You've got that golden-retriever energy."

He smiles. "Golden what?"

"Golden retriever. You know, in romance books—" But I stop. Because I'm not a romance writer anymore and I don't want to explain these things to him.

"Oh, right," he says. "Yeah. I've heard of that."

"Heard of *what*?" I scoff.

"Tropes. Dark romance."

"*What*?" My mouth is hanging open.

"What? Why are you looking at me that way? I stumbled into Booktok one day last year and…" he blows out a breath. "Never quite recovered from what I saw."

Now… I'm intrigued. My voice lowers too. "What did you see?"

Marty shifts in his seat. His fingers drum the table again,

then stop. He looks down at his salad like it might save him from this conversation.

"I mean—" He clears his throat. "I saw... videos. Of women talking about books. Dark romance books. Really dark ones."

I just stare at him.

"Like, not the billionaire CEO kind of dark. Not the 'he's brooding but secretly has a heart of gold' dark." His voice drops lower. "The... the *actually* dark kind."

My mouth falls open.

Marty's face is flushing now. Red creeping up his neck. "The kidnapping kind. The—the Stockholm syndrome kind. The—" He stops. Swallows hard. "The kind where the guy is legitimately fucked up and does fucked up things and the woman—"

He can't finish the sentence.

I lean forward. "And the woman what?"

"Wants it anyway." The words come out strangled. "Even though she shouldn't. Even though it's wrong. Even though every part of her knows it's wrong but she—she still—"

He cuts himself off, breathing harder now.

"You watched videos about that?" My voice sounds strange. Distant.

"I fell down a rabbit hole." He's looking anywhere but at me. "For like... three months. Just watching these women talk about their favorite dark romance books. About mafia bosses, and stalkers, and—and monsters. Literal monsters sometimes. And they'd get this look in their eyes when they talked about it. This... this *need*."

My pussy clenches.

Just once.

But I feel it.

Marty finally looks at me. "So I'm asking. What's your type, Scarletta?"

I open my mouth to answer, but nothing comes out.

My brain is scrambling. Trying to construct something. Anything.

What's my type?

The question should be simple. It's not.

Marty watches me for another few seconds, then sighs heavily and leans back in the booth.

"Never mind. Forget I asked." He picks up his fork, stabbing at his salad with more force than necessary. "You're not my type anyway."

My stomach drops. "What?"

"I mean—" He shrugs, not looking at me. "You're too independent. Too... strong. I can tell just from talking to you for like twenty minutes. You've got your shit together. Your own career. Your own apartment. You don't *need* anyone."

The words hit wrong. Like he's describing someone else entirely.

"I like—" He stops. Clears his throat. "I prefer more demure women. Quieter. Softer. Women who actually want to be taken care of instead of..." He gestures vaguely at me.

I should feel insulted.

I don't.

Because heat is pooling between my legs. Slow and insistent.

Demure. Softer. Women who want to be taken care of.

"I'm only asking because I don't want to waste your time." Marty's still not looking at me, just pushing lettuce around his plate. "Or mine, honestly. I know that sounds shitty but I'm just—I'm desperate to find someone I can actually connect with. Someone who wants what I want. And you clearly don't."

My face is burning now. My thighs press together under the table.

I try to speak. "I—I might—"

"It's a stupid question anyway." He cuts me off, waving his hand dismissively. "Forget it."

But I can't forget it.

Because my pussy is throbbing. Actually *throbbing* for the first time in six months.

"No." My voice comes out strangled. "Tell me."

Marty looks up. "What?"

"Tell me exactly what you were thinking." I lean forward, my hands flat on the table. "What you want. Maybe I—maybe I might be up for it."

His eyes narrow slightly. Studying me.

Then he sets down his fork very deliberately.

He leans in.

His voice drops so low I have to strain to hear it over the ambient noise of the restaurant.

"I want to fuck a woman's throat until she can't breathe."

My breath catches.

Marty's gaze locks onto mine. Doesn't waver.

"Not gently. Not carefully. I want to grab her hair—really *grab* it, hard enough to hurt—and hold her head exactly where I want it while I use her mouth like it's just another hole for me to fill."

Oh god.

"I want her on her knees. Hands behind her back because I don't want her touching me, I don't want her having any control at all. I want her completely helpless while I push my cock so deep down her throat that she gags, and chokes, and her eyes water."

My clit is pulsing.

"I want to feel her throat convulse around me when she can't take it anymore. I want to hear those desperate little sounds she makes when she's trying to breathe but can't because I'm too far down. I want to watch mascara run down her face while she struggles."

I'm wet.

Actually *wet*.

Marty doesn't stop.

"And when she thinks I'm going to pull out and let her breathe, I want to push in even deeper instead. I want to hold her there—hold her head against my pelvis with my cock buried completely—until she's panicking. Until her hands are clawing at my thighs. Until she's genuinely terrified I'm not going to let her up."

His eyes are burning into mine.

"Then I want to pull out just long enough for her to gasp one breath before I shove back in and do it all over again. Harder. Rougher. Until her throat is raw and her jaw aches and she's sobbing around my cock."

Holy fuck.

"I want to come down her throat while she's still choking on it. I want to hold her there until she swallows every drop even though she's gagging and desperate for air. And then when I finally pull out, I want to watch her collapse on the floor gasping and crying while I tell her what a good girl she was for taking it."

Marty leans back slowly.

His expression hasn't changed. Still that calm, focused intensity.

"That's what I was thinking."

I'm staring at him.

My mouth is open. My face is burning. My pussy is soaked.

He could write scenes.

Like... he could actually write the kind of scenes I write.

Wrote.

Past tense.

But sitting here listening to him describe throat-fucking in explicit, filthy detail while maintaining perfect eye contact—

Maybe this could work.

Maybe Marty isn't some spineless beta after all.

I'm staring at Marty and my brain is shorting out.

He's attractive. Like, actually *attractive* now that he's not doing the wholesome yoga instructor routine. Now that I know what's underneath the golden retriever exterior.

His hands. God, his hands are big. Long fingers. Strong wrists. The kind of hands that could—

I imagine them fisted in my hair. The way he'd hold my head still. Not gentle. Not asking permission.

My thighs press together harder.

What does his cock look like?

The thought crashes through me unbidden. Vivid. Desperate.

He's tall. Six-two, maybe six-three. And guys that tall are usually proportional, right? Thick. Long. The kind of cock that would stretch my jaw. The kind I'd struggle to fit.

I imagine kneeling in front of him. His hands gripping my hair while he feeds his dick between my lips inch by inch. How tight my throat would feel when he pushed deeper. How I'd gag, and choke, and he wouldn't stop. Wouldn't pull back. Wouldn't ask if I'm okay.

He'd just keep going.

My pussy clenches so hard I have to bite back a sound.

I open my mouth.

"I—"

"I can't do this."

Marty's voice cracks. He's shaking his head, hands coming up to run through his hair.

"This is too weird. I can't—" He laughs, but it's wrong. Strangled. "I can't believe I agreed to this."

I go completely still.

Something in my chest stops moving.

"Marty—"

"No, I'm sorry. I'm really sorry." He's not looking at me anymore. His eyes are darting around the restaurant like he's searching for an exit. "I shouldn't have—fuck, this was such a bad idea."

My hands are flat on the table. I don't move them.

"What was a bad idea?"

He winces. Actually *winces* like I slapped him.

"This. The whole—" He gestures between us. "The date. The conversation. All of it."

The floor drops out from under me.

"Someone put you up to this."

It's not a question. I already know.

Marty's face crumples. "I didn't want to—I mean, I needed the money. My studio, the pottery thing, it's not making any profit, and my parents are threatening to pull funding, and I'm gonna lose everything. The lease, the equipment, all of it. And this guy, he just—he offered me so much money to take you out and say those things and I thought, fuck, how hard could it be? Just have dinner with some girl and talk dirty for an hour."

My throat is closing. "What guy."

"I don't know his name." Marty's rambling now, words spilling out in a panicked rush. "He wouldn't tell me. He just calls himself—"

He stops.

Swallows.

"The Masked Man."

Everything inside me shrivels.

Dies.

Turns to ash.

The Masked Man.

Caleb.

Of course it's Caleb.

Of course he's still watching. Still manipulating. Still pulling strings like I'm his fucking puppet.

I can't breathe.

Marty is still talking. "He gave me a script. Like, literally word-for-word what to say. The BookTok thing, the throat-fucking thing, all of it. He said you'd respond to it. That you'd get turned on if I said it right. And I—god, I'm such an asshole. I actually practiced in the mirror."

My vision is blurring at the edges.

"He told me to come on strong. Said he knew exactly what would make you wet. Those were his literal words. My god, what the fuck is wrong with me? But I was like, how hard could it be? Ya know?"

Stop talking.

Please stop talking.

"But then, I was sitting here watching you react—watching your face when I said those things—" Marty's voice breaks again. "You actually believed it. You thought I meant it. And that's so fucked up. That's so—"

He stands abruptly.

I don't look up.

Marty pulls out his wallet. Bills hit the table. I count them in my peripheral vision. Five hundred-dollar bills.

"That's his money," Marty says. "The Masked Man's. You can keep the change or whatever. I don't—I can't—"

He's backing away. "I'm sorry. I know that doesn't mean anything but I'm really, really sorry."

And then he's gone.

Walking away.

Leaving me sitting here alone.

The restaurant noise floods back in. Conversations. Silverware clinking. Someone laughing at a nearby table.

I'm still frozen.

Still not breathing right.

Five hundred dollars is sitting in front of me.

The Masked Man's money.

Caleb's money.

He scripted Marty.

He gave him lines about throat-fucking, and control, and demure women who need to be taken care of.

He knew exactly what would make me wet after six months of no contact.

He knew exactly how to break me down.

And I fell for it.

I actually *fell for it.*

My hands are shaking.

I look down at them spread flat on the table and I don't recognize them as mine.

The pizza sits half-eaten on my plate.

Marty's salad is still there across from me, abandoned.

Five hundred dollars in cash.

You can keep the change.

Like I'm a waitress.

Like I'm something he can tip on his way out.

I don't move.

Can't move.

I just sit here.

Staring at the money.

Feeling the wetness between my thighs start to cool.

Feeling my arousal drain away and leave nothing but hollow shame in its place.

He knew exactly what would make you wet.

And he was right.

CHAPTER 4
CALEB

It was predictable, this reaction—entirely, completely, boringly predictable.

I didn't choose Marty on accident. Every decision I make is calculated. Weighed and measured against a dozen variables until I know exactly what outcome to expect.

I didn't miscalculate how he would react to his assignment, didn't misjudge his character or overestimate his spine.

He's a twenty-two-year-old Jackson Hole trust-fund brat who spent every single formative year of his privileged little life learning how to roll over and show his belly.

The kind of kid who inherited more money than sense when he turned eighteen and immediately proved he had no idea what to do with either.

What kind of eighteen-year-old buys a pottery business with their trust fund? What kind of kid looks at millions of dollars in liquid assets and thinks, "You know what Idaho Falls needs? Another artisanal ceramics studio."

Marty, that's who. Marty with his expensive fleece vests, and his earnest expressions, and his complete inability to say no to anyone with even a whisper of authority in their voice.

He was absolutely perfect for this assignment.

Immediately after he leaves the pizzeria, my phone starts blowing up with texts.

Srry man

coulnt do it

im out

I'm not even annoyed that he told Scarletta the truth—though I admit I wasn't entirely certain that would be how this played out. There was always the possibility he'd follow through, that his need for my approval would outweigh whatever nascent moral compass he pretends to navigate by.

But no. He cracked. Folded like wet cardboard under the slightest pressure of her direct, unflinching stare.

Now she knows.

Now. *She knows.*

I'm sitting in my Tahoe across the street from the pizzeria, engine off, windows tinted dark enough that no one walking past would even register my presence. But I'm not watching the street. I'm watching Scarletta on the dash display—a custom setup I had installed last month, three high-definition screens mounted seamlessly into the console, each one capable of cycling through every camera feed I currently have access to in Idaho Falls.

Right now, all three screens are locked on her.

I watch her sit perfectly still for forty-three seconds.

Not frozen—there's a distinction I've learned to recognize through almost a year of surveillance footage. Frozen means the body locks while the mind scrambles. This is different.

She's choosing to remain motionless.

Her chest rises and falls in slow, measured breaths. Her hands rest flat on the table on either side of the abandoned pizza. Her gaze fixed somewhere in the middle distance, not tracking Marty's retreating form, not examining the five hundred-dollar bills he left behind like an apology he couldn't voice.

Just... sitting.

I zoom the feed slightly, adjusting the angle. The camera I have control of inside the restaurant, courtesy of a hack into their pathetic security system, gives me a perfect three-quarter view. I can see her profile, the line of her throat, the way her jaw tightens almost imperceptibly.

She's thinking.

Processing.

And I know exactly what she's processing because I designed this entire scenario to force her into this exact mental state.

He's still watching.

He knows where I am.

He knows what turns me on.

He paid someone to say those specific words.

The thoughts probably aren't that articulate—trauma and arousal don't produce linear thinking—but the core realizations are landing. I can see them registering in the subtle shift of her shoulders, the way her fingers curl slightly against the laminate tabletop.

Fifty-one seconds now.

A waitress approaches, says something I can't hear. Scarletta doesn't respond immediately. The waitress lingers, awkward, probably asking if everything's okay, if she needs anything, standard hospitality script.

Scarletta's lips move. Short response. The waitress retreats.

Fifty-eight seconds.

Then she moves.

Not dramatically. Not a panic response or a flight reaction. She simply picks up one of the hundred-dollar bills Marty left, places it deliberately on top of the check, and stands.

Leaves the other four hundred dollars sitting there.

Interesting.

She walks toward the exit with the same measured control she maintained while sitting—back straight, steps even, face carefully neutral. Someone who didn't know her might think she's perfectly composed.

But I know her.

I know the way her fingers flex at her sides means she's fighting the urge to ball them into fists. I know the slight tension in her jaw means she's clenching her teeth. I know the deliberate pace means she's forcing herself not to run.

She exits the pizzeria and turns left down the sidewalk.

Not toward her apartment—that's the opposite direction.

She's walking deeper into downtown, which means she hasn't decided where she's going yet. She's moving because staying still felt dangerous, but she hasn't formed a plan beyond *get away from here*.

I switch camera feeds, cycling through the network I have positioned throughout her regular routes. She appears on the next screen—different angle, same controlled stride. I watch her pass the bookstore she never enters, the wine bar she's been to twice with yoga dates who bored her.

Her phone is in her purse. I know because I saw her stuff it in there as she entered the pizzeria for her date.

She hasn't pulled it out yet.

Hasn't called anyone, hasn't texted anyone, hasn't opened her banking app to check if more money appeared like magic the way it did after Christmas. The way it has every week since Valentine's Day.

Scarletta Mae Desmond has several million dollars in a slew of bank accounts all across the Rocky Mountains. I doubt she has any idea what her net worth is at this moment.

She's got no sense of money at all. She didn't even file taxes.

It's fine, though. I did that for her. Just like I do everything for her. Unaware, unappreciated, don't care.

She's walking, and thinking, and probably spiraling. And I'm sitting in my Tahoe across the street from where she just was, watching her move through my city like she still believes she has privacy.

Like she still believes I'm not everywhere she goes outside her new apartment.

The arousal from watching this is different than what I felt watching her in the old apartment. Or with the attendants. Or any other time, actually. It's entirely different than any experience I've had with her so far.

This isn't about her body surrendering to physical stimulation she can't control.

This is about her mind.

Right now, Scarletta is realizing—truly, fully realizing—that six months of silence from me didn't mean I went away. It meant I was letting her think she could build a life without me while I watched every single attempt.

Every coffee shop writing session where she stared at blank documents.

Every gym workout where she went through motions without purpose.

Every yoga class where she met nice men with gentle hands who couldn't give her what she needs.

I watched all of it.

And now she *knows* I watched all of it.

She stops walking.

Middle of the sidewalk, no clear destination, just... stops.

She turns around in a slow circle. Looking everywhere at once. Scanning, searching.

For me.

Then… she begins to scream.

Not panic scream, actual, articulate words.

"You motherfucker!" It comes out loud.

People stop, stare, laugh.

"You sick, sadistic, creepy, fucked-up motherfucker! I know you're watching me!"

Well, that was perfect.

Everyone in the vicinity has now labeled her.

Psycho.

She's still screaming.

"You think this is *romantic*? You think paying some fucking —some yoga bro to recite lines at me like I'm a character in one of my own goddamn stories is—"

A couple walking past crosses to the other side of the street.

Smart.

"—is what? Proof you *understand* me? Proof you *know* me?"

Her voice cracks on that last word, and something hot and visceral tightens in my chest.

Yes.

Yes, that's exactly what it means.

"You're a fucking *stalker*!" She spins again, arms spread wide, addressing the entire downtown corridor like she's performing for an audience she can't see. "A murderer! A psychopath who gets off on—"

She stops herself.

She's not stupid enough to say *what* I get off on. Not out loud.

"—on controlling people!" She finishes instead, breathing hard. "On manipulating them into thinking they want things they don't actually want!"

A man in a business suit pauses near the corner, phone already out. Probably deciding whether this constitutes a 911-worthy public disturbance or just another downtown crazy.

I zoom the feed tighter on Scarletta's face.

Her cheeks are flushed. Eyes bright. Chest heaving with each ragged breath.

She's *furious*.

And she's *alive*.

For the first time in six months of surveillance footage, she looks genuinely, viscerally *present* in her own body instead of performing existence for invisible judges who've already convicted her.

"I *destroyed* your cameras!" Her voice goes shrill on that word. "I deleted everything! I left! I *left*, and you were supposed to—you were supposed to just—"

Let you go?

Is that what she thought?

That I'd orchestrate months of elaborate psychological seduction, spend literal millions of dollars creating experiences tailored specifically to her darkest fantasies, confess to multiple homicides, and then just... what?

Move on?

Find another broken girl who writes prettily about her own destruction?

The business suit guy is definitely calling someone now. Probably not 911—he doesn't look concerned enough—but security, maybe. Downtown has private patrols that deal with public disturbances.

I should feel something about that. Concern, maybe. Strategic recalibration.

Instead, I'm just watching her.

"You don't get to do this!" She's crying now, tears streaming, and she doesn't bother wiping them away. "You don't get to—to *leave* me alone for six months and then—"

She stops.

Realizes what she just said.

Her mouth opens. Closes.

Leave me alone.

As in: you abandoned me, and I hated it, and now you're back and I hate that too.

I see the exact moment she hears her own words the way I heard them.

Her expression shifts. Closes down. The fury drains out of her posture like someone pulled a plug, and suddenly she's just a girl standing on a sidewalk in downtown Idaho Falls, crying in public while strangers stare.

She looks smaller.

Defeated.

She wipes her face with the back of her hand, smearing mascara across her cheek. Straightens her shoulders. Takes one long, shaky breath that I can see even through the camera feed.

Then she looks directly at the camera positioned above the bookstore entrance.

She can't possibly know which one I'm using. There are seven feeds covering this block alone.

But she's looking right at it anyway.

"Fuck you," she says clearly. Quietly. Just loud enough for the microphone to catch. "Fuck you, Caleb."

The business suit guy definitely heard that. He's looking at her differently now—not crazy lady, but someone who knows a specific person's name. Someone with a story.

Scarletta turns and walks away.

Not running. Not fleeing.

Just... walking.

Back toward her apartment, finally. Toward safety. Toward the only space she thinks I can't reach anymore.

I watch until she turns the corner and disappears from the downtown camera coverage.

Then I sit back in the driver's seat, hands resting on the steering wheel, and smile.

Finally.

Six months of watching her pretend.

Six months of controlled routines and careful performance.

Six months of her trying to convince herself—and me—that she's moved on.

And it took one scripted date with a trust fund pottery boy to shatter the entire illusion.

She's thinking about me again.

Screaming about me again.

Saying my name like a curse she can't stop speaking.

The pretending is over—

A sharp knock on my window.

I turn my head and actually laugh.

She's here. She found me.

She knocks again, harder this time. "I know you're in there, you sick fuck!"

She found me.

She found me.

I lower the window.

And she *explodes*.

"You sick fuck—you absolute piece of shit—you think this is *funny*? You think watching me lose my mind on a public street is *entertainment*?"

The words pour out of her like water from a broken dam. No filter. No performance. Just raw, uncut fury.

"Stalker—predator—manipulative   psychopath—you killed someone, you *murdered* someone and jerked off on their corpse and I *saw* you and you think—you actually think—"

She's not making complete sentences anymore. Just fragments. Shrapnel.

"—that I'd want anything to do with you after—after everything you—controlling freak—obsessive—*insane*—"

My cock is already hard.

Not just hard. Throbbing. Aching. Straining against my zipper while she calls me every name she can summon from whatever dark vocabulary she's been building during six months of pretending I don't exist.

"—pathetic excuse for a man who has to *buy* women because no one would ever willingly—"

I open the door.

She jumps back, mid-rant, eyes going wide.

I unfold myself from the driver's seat, standing to my full

height. She has to tilt her head back to maintain eye contact, and I watch her throat work as she swallows.

But she doesn't stop talking.

"Don't you dare—don't you fucking dare come near me, I will scream, I will call the police, I will—"

I lean down until my lips are at her ear.

"Follow me, my good little slut."

Then I walk away.

Don't look back. Don't check if she's following. Don't give her the satisfaction of seeing uncertainty.

I head toward the alley between the bookstore and the wine bar—narrow, shadowed, exactly the kind of space decent people avoid after dark.

The alley smells like piss and rotting food from the dumpster halfway down. Not romantic. Not curated. Not part of any fantasy I've written for her.

Just real.

Just what's available right now.

I walk past the dumpster, past the rusted fire escape, to the alcove where the buildings don't quite meet—a gap maybe four feet wide, tucked behind a broken downspout.

I turn.

There she is.

Standing at the mouth of the alcove, breathing hard, mascara streaked down both cheeks.

Watching me.

I reach for my belt.

Her eyes drop immediately. Track every movement of my fingers as I unbuckle. As I unbutton. As I lower the zipper.

When I pull out my cock—already fully erect, already leaking—she licks her lips.

Unconscious gesture. Pure instinct.

Her eyes stay locked on my hand as I stroke myself once. Twice.

Then she looks up. Meets my gaze.

"Come here," I say quietly.

She doesn't move.

"Now, Scarletta."

One step. Then another. Hesitant. Like she's approaching something dangerous.

Smart girl.

"Press your back against that wall."

I gesture to the filthy brick behind me. Graffiti tags layered over years. Stains I don't want to identify. Rough texture that will scratch exposed skin.

Anger flashes in her eyes.

Good.

I want her angry. Want her conscious of every choice she makes. Want her to remember she walked into this alley knowing exactly what I'd ask for.

What I'd demand.

She moves past me into the alcove. The space is so narrow our bodies brush as she passes, and I hear her breath catch.

Then she turns.

Presses her back against the brick wall.

Just stands there.

Waiting.

I stroke my cock slowly, deliberately, letting her watch.

Her chest rises and falls in rapid, shallow breaths. Her pupils are blown wide. Her hands flatten against the brick on either side of her hips—not pushing off, not trying to leave.

Just bracing.

"Six months," I say conversationally, still stroking. "Six months of watching you pretend."

Her jaw tightens.

"Watching you run every morning like you're training for something. Watching you sit in that coffee shop staring at blank documents. Watching you go on dates with boring men who couldn't fuck you the way you need if their lives depended on it."

"Fuck you," she whispers.

"You will," I agree. "But not yet."

I step closer.

Close enough that the head of my cock nearly brushes her stomach through that pretty yellow sundress she's wearing. Fabric so thin I can see the outline of her hip bones beneath it. Summer dress that screams *wholesome* and *normal* and *definitely not the kind of girl who writes rape fantasies in her spare time.*

She doesn't move away.

Her breathing picks up. Shallow, rapid. I can see her pulse hammering in her throat.

"How'd you like Marty?" I ask, genuinely curious. My hand keeps moving on my cock. "Was he the kind of safe man you were looking for?"

Her eyes flick down to my hand. Back up to my face. Defiant.

"Did he meet your expectations?" I tilt my head, studying her flushed cheeks. "Did you imagine what it would feel like, pretty slut? His nice, respectful cock inside you? The way he'd probably ask permission before every single thing he did to your body?"

"Stop," she whispers.

But she's not looking at my eyes when she says it. She's watching my hand stroke my cock. Watching precum leak from the tip.

"Do you still masturbate?" I ask casually. "Or did you give that up too when you decided to play normal?"

Something flashes across her face. Shame, maybe. Or anger at being seen.

"You already know I don't," she says flatly. "You've been watching me."

I shake my head slowly. "Not in your apartment. I understand limits, Scarletta. You destroyed the cameras. I respected that boundary."

She actually laughs. A sharp, bitter sound that cuts through the space between us. "Limits?" She stares at me like I've said something genuinely hilarious. "*Limits*? You're standing in an alley jerking off in front of me and you want credit for respecting boundaries?"

Fair point.

I press my cock against her stomach. Just the head at first. Light pressure. Enough that she feels it through the thin fabric.

A wet spot blooms on the yellow cotton. Clear fluid soaking into the dress. Marking her.

"Why don't you masturbate anymore?" I ask quietly. "What happened?"

"Fuck off." Her voice shakes. "It's none of your business. And if you think it is—if you think that money you keep sending me is enough to buy me again—you're mistaken."

I don't answer.

Just keep stroking myself. Slower now. Deliberate. Watching her watch me.

Then I press forward again.

This time I don't stop. I rub my cock against her dress in slow, deliberate circles. Smearing precum across the yellow fabric. Soiling it on purpose. Claiming it.

Ruining it.

Her eyes stay locked on mine.

She's holding her breath.

I can see her ribs expand and freeze. Can see the way her lips part slightly like she's about to speak but can't quite form words.

"Make me stop," I say softly.

She doesn't move.

"Say the word, Scarletta. Tell me no. Push me away. Scream for help." I press my thigh between her legs. "Do any single fucking thing that indicates you don't want this."

A whimper escapes her throat.

Small sound. Desperate.

I move my thigh. Slow, firm pressure against her pussy through the dress. Rubbing her the way I know she needs. The way those boring yoga instructors and pottery boys never could.

"That's what I thought," I murmur. "Still just a filthy little slut who gets wet when dangerous men corner her in alleys."

"No—" She gasps when I increase the pressure. "I'm not—"

"You are." I keep grinding my thigh against her pussy. Feel the heat of her through two layers of fabric. "You're a desperate, cock-hungry whore who's been pretending to be normal for six months and hating every second of it."

Another whimper.

Her hands are still pressed flat against the brick wall, but her hips have started moving. Small, unconscious rocks forward into the friction I'm providing.

"That's right, pretty slut," I breathe. "Take what you need. Hump my leg like the bitch in heat you are."

"Stop—" But she doesn't mean it. Her body is betraying every protest her mouth makes.

"You want to come, don't you?" I watch her face. The flush spreading down her neck. The way her eyes keep losing focus. "You want to soak through this nice wholesome dress while I watch. Want to prove you're still the same broken girl who checked all those boxes on a consent form because she needed someone to own her."

She's close.

I can read every sign. The way her breathing hitches. The tension building in her shoulders. The desperate little sounds catching in her throat.

So I stop moving.

Step back.

Remove all contact.

Her eyes fly open. Wild. Devastated.

"No—" It comes out broken. "Please—"

She catches herself. Claps both hands over her mouth like she can shove the word back inside.

But I heard it.

Please.

She's trembling. Tears streaming down her face now, mixing with the smeared mascara. She turns away from me, pressing her face into her hands.

Trying to hide.

I reach out. Gentle this time. Thread my fingers through her hair the way I know she likes—firm enough to feel controlled, soft enough to feel safe.

"All you have to do is ask," I whisper directly into her ear. "Say the word and I'll put my big cock up inside that needy pussy of yours. Fuck you right here against this dirty wall until you scream. Give you everything you've been dreaming about for six months."

She lifts her head.

Looks at me with those tear-bright eyes.

Parts her lips.

"Please, Master."

Victory surges through me—

Then she shoves past me. Hard enough that I actually stumble.

"Please, Master," she repeats, voice dripping venom. "Go fuck yourself."

She tries to walk away.

I grab her arm.

Not hard. Just enough to stop her momentum. Just enough to turn her back toward me.

I knew it would end like this the first time. Knew she'd bolt the moment she felt herself surrendering.

So I prepared.

I pull the business card from my pocket. Heavy card stock, embossed lettering. My real contact information—not some burner number, not a proxy.

Direct access.

I hold it up so she can see it. Read the name printed there in elegant serif font. Then I slip it into her purse. "You know where to find me," I say calmly, "when you're ready for this cock again."

I tuck myself back into my slacks. Take my time with the zipper. The button. The belt.

Let her watch me compose myself while she stands there, flushed, and desperate, and furious.

Then I turn and walk away.

"I won't be back, Scarletta," I call over my shoulder. Let my voice carry through the alley. Let her hear the absolute certainty in it.

"You *will* come to me."

CHAPTER 5
SCARLETTA

I'm staring at my ceiling. Again.

The words won't stop this time. They're flying through my head like they used to—back when writing felt like breathing instead of drowning. Ivy and Logan. The sex club. The bench. The crowd.

I dreamt about them last night.

Actual dreams. Not the blank nothing I've been swimming through for six months. Not the dissociative fog where I wake up and can't remember if I slept or just stopped existing for eight hours.

Real, vivid, filthy dreams.

I close my eyes. Slip my fingers between my legs.

I'm already wet.

Jesus Christ.

I haven't been wet like this since—

No. Not thinking about that. Not thinking about him.

Just Ivy and Logan. Just the story.

Inside Logan's sex club, Ivy is bent over a bench facing a crowd of people. Most of them are naked—like completely naked. Hard cocks everywhere. Tits everywhere. Glistening pussies. Bodies pressed together, watching, waiting.

They're eagerly awaiting Ivy's scene debut.

She knows there are mirrors positioned behind her. Angled perfectly so the people in front can see what Logan is going to do. Can watch his fingers spread her open. Can see how wet she is. How her pussy clenches around nothing, desperate and needy and—

Logan steps behind her. His hand slides up her inner thigh.

Except it's not Logan anymore.

It's Caleb.

I don't even try to stop it. Don't pretend I'm still writing fiction.

I'm in Ivy's position now. Bent over that bench. Spread wide. Mirrors behind me reflecting everything for the crowd to see.

And Caleb's fingers—those expert, ruthless fingers that know exactly how to make me fall apart—slide through my wetness.

"Look at you," his voice echoes in my head. Low. Commanding. "Dripping for all these strangers to see."

My actual fingers circle my clit. Clumsy compared to his. Desperate compared to his control.

But God, I'm so wet.

"Such a good little slut," Caleb whispers in my fantasy. His finger pushes inside me. Just one. Slow. "Putting on a show. Letting everyone watch what a filthy whore you are."

I arch on my bed. Push two fingers inside myself.

The crowd in my head is watching. Stroking themselves. Getting off on watching Caleb finger-fuck me in front of them.

"Please—" I hear myself beg in the fantasy. "Please, Master—"

The orgasm hits me like a physical blow.

I'm writhing. Making sounds I don't recognize—high,

desperate, obscene noises that bounce off these expensive high ceilings and fill my sterile apartment with proof of exactly what I am.

A broken girl who can only come when she imagines the man who stalked her.

The man who killed someone in front of her.

The man who—

Another wave crashes through me and I'm gasping, my fingers working frantically, chasing every last pulse of pleasure until I'm shaking and my thighs are trembling and I can't breathe.

I collapse back against my expensive sheets.

Stare at my expensive ceiling.

Seven times.

I've masturbated seven times since I left him in that alley last night.

Seven incredible orgasms.

After six months of nothing. Six months of my body refusing to respond to anything—not fantasies, not porn, not the battery-powered vibrator I spent two hundred dollars on in a moment of desperate hope.

Nothing worked.

Until yesterday. Until he pressed his thigh between my legs in a dirty alley and called me a filthy slut and my entire body woke up screaming *yes*.

I should be horrified.

I *am* horrified.

But I'm also—

God.

I press my wet fingers against my mouth. Taste myself.

The way he made me do. That first time. When he fingered me and then made me suck his fingers clean while he called me a good girl.

My pussy clenches.

I could go again. Right now. I could slip my hand back

between my legs and come an eighth time just thinking about—

No.

I force myself to sit up. Swing my legs over the side of the bed.

My thighs are sticky. The sheets are damp beneath me.

Evidence.

I stumble to the bathroom. Turn the shower on scalding hot.

While the water heats, I catch my reflection in the mirror.

Flushed. Hair a mess. Pupils blown wide.

I look like I've been thoroughly fucked.

Except I haven't been. I've just been lying in bed alone, getting myself off to memories of a man who gets turned on by torture.

After my shower, I find myself lingering in the apartment, wandering aimlessly from the bathroom to the kitchen and back again.

Usually, I can't wait to get the fuck out of here as soon as I'm dressed—I've developed this restless, caged feeling the moment I wake up. Like the walls are closing in.

I used to be afraid of the outside world. Used to love my solitary lifestyle, actually. The quiet. The isolation. The way I could disappear into my own head for days at a time without anyone noticing or caring.

I used to tell myself I enjoyed the loneliness—that it was a choice, not a circumstance.

Well, that's not really true, is it?

Maybe I didn't exactly *enjoy* being lonely, but I was comfortable in it. Familiar with it. It was like an old, worn-out sweater that didn't fit quite right but you kept wearing anyway because at least you knew what to expect.

And besides, I had my writing. My stories. My online community of faceless readers who didn't know my real name or see my real face.

That made it bearable.

More than bearable—it gave me purpose.

That all changed after I came home from the island.

Everything changed.

I couldn't stand to be alone anymore. Couldn't stand to be in that apartment with its four walls closing in and the silence pressing down like a physical weight. Couldn't write a single fucking word, no matter how many times I opened my laptop and stared at the blinking cursor.

The stories that used to flow out of me—dark, twisted, cathartic—they just... stopped.

So... the first thing I did was start looking for a new apartment.

I needed to get out of that studio. Needed walls that didn't hold memories of *before*—before the island, before him, before everything got so goddamn complicated. I couldn't write there anymore. Couldn't breathe there. Every corner reminded me of the person I used to be, the one who thought she had her life figured out even when it was falling apart.

The application process for rentals these days is *insane*. Background checks, credit checks, employment verification, references. I didn't qualify for anything—not with my credit score in the toilet and my employment history looking like a fucking patchwork quilt of part-time gigs and freelance work that barely covered rent.

But for this place—this beautiful, enormous third-floor loft with its exposed brick and twelve-foot ceilings and windows that let in actual goddamn sunlight—I offered to pay a year in advance.

Thirty thousand dollars.

Cash. Well, wire transfer. Same difference.

I didn't even blink when I made the offer.

The landlord didn't either. Just nodded like people threw that kind of money around every day and handed me the keys three days later.

Nine months ago, I'd never had thirty thousand dollars in my life. Hell, I doubt I even *made* that in a year with the pathetic employment history I had—cobbling together coffee shop shifts, and freelance copywriting gigs that paid pennies, and restaurant work that left me smelling like fryer grease.

Now, I literally have millions.

I don't know the exact number. I stopped trying to calculate it after the first few weeks.

Every month I get bank statements in my email. Each account has exactly two hundred fifty thousand dollars in it. No more, no less. The maximum the FDIC covers in case of bank failure.

I had to look that up. I didn't understand why he kept making new accounts instead of just dumping everything into one. Why the specific number. Why it mattered.

Finally ChatGPT explained it to me in tiny little baby words: federal insurance limits, asset protection, risk mitigation. The kind of financial planning that people with actual wealth do automatically, without even thinking about it.

I don't know how many accounts there are. A dozen, at least. Maybe more.

I don't even open those emails anymore.

I have enough money to really escape. To actually, genuinely disappear if I wanted to badly enough. The resources are there, sitting in those accounts I don't open anymore, waiting to be deployed.

I could hire someone to help me cover my tracks—a fixer, maybe, whatever those people are called. Probably hire an entire security team if I needed to. Find a hacker who specializes in making people vanish digitally. Get myself somewhere safe, somewhere remote. Purchase a whole new identity with papers good enough to pass scrutiny. Figure out a way to systematically close all those accounts he set up, liquidate everything, and funnel it into new ones under a different name in a different country.

I've thought about it. Late at night when I can't sleep, when the walls of this beautiful apartment feel like a new prison, just prettier. I've mapped it out in my head, step by step, like plotting one of my stories.

The logistics of disappearing.

There are exactly two reasons I don't do this.

One. Deep down, in the part of me that's learned to think like him whether I wanted to or not, I don't think it would actually work.

Whatever money I have access to—these millions that still don't feel real, that I can't quite wrap my head around—he's got a billion times more than that.

Literally.

His resources outweigh mine so completely it's almost laughable to compare them. The power differential is staggering.

If he genuinely wants to find me, if I become a problem he needs to solve, he will find me. He'll deploy whatever tools, whatever people, whatever technology it takes.

And unlike me fumbling around trying to figure out how disappearing even works, he'd know exactly how to do it efficiently.

And two… and this is the part that makes me hate myself a little more each time I acknowledge it… I don't actually *want* to leave.

Not him, not this place, not even this completely fucked-up scenario we're living in.

It's… God, it's exciting. It makes me feel alive in a way nothing else ever has.

It's also sick. Deeply, fundamentally sick.

And I'm so goddamn tired of being sick.

This changes today.

At the airport, standing in the check-in line with my single carry-on bag, I have second thoughts.

Is it crazy to fly to Vegas to shop?

Yes. I mean, there's no other answer than yes, is there?

That's the rational response. The sensible one. The thing a normal person would say if you told them what I'm doing right now—booking a last-minute flight to Nevada because I've decided the boutiques in Idaho Falls aren't going to cut it for whatever this transformation is supposed to be.

But… if one had the funds—and I do, courtesy of Caleb's relentless deposits that keep appearing in my account like accusations I haven't responded to—and one had never been to Vegas, which I haven't, and one was shopping for a glow-up, which is apparently what I'm calling this performance now, and one lived in sleepy Idaho Falls where the most exciting store is a Target that still has a Pizza Hut inside it… is it really crazy?

The woman ahead of me in line checks two massive suitcases and I wonder where she's going, if it's somewhere normal, somewhere that makes sense. I adjust my grip on my bag and don't move when the line shifts forward.

I need a change.

Not just a trim or a new lipstick shade or one of those magazine makeover articles that promises transformation in five easy steps. Not a tiny change. A massive change. The kind that turns you into someone else entirely—someone you can pretend to be until maybe, eventually, you forget you were ever anyone different.

I need advice about this change too. Professional advice. Like, actual cut-and-color expertise from someone who went to school for this, who knows what they're doing, who can look at me and see potential instead of the girl who's been wearing the same oversized hoodie rotation for the past two years.

Someone who can work miracles with highlights, and layers, and whatever else people pay for at real salons.

And not just hair advice either—I need the whole package. The full Pretty Woman treatment, the complete before-and-after transformation montage where the frumpy nobody walks into the boutique and walks out looking like she belongs in a different tax bracket.

Because I do belong there now. In that different tax bracket, with all the women who smell like expensive perfume, and have skin that glows from regular facials, and bodies maintained by personal trainers.

Who cares if I didn't earn it the normal way—and objectively, didn't I earn it? I mean, what the fuck, right? After everything that happened, after the island and the cabin and watching him—no. Not thinking about that. But still. If anyone's earned the right to spend money they didn't technically work for in any traditional sense, it's me.

I'm not poor, dirty, sick Scarletta anymore. I'm not the girl who wore the same leggings for four days straight because laundry felt impossible. I'm not the one who forgot to eat, who lived on instant ramen and black coffee, who couldn't afford a haircut.

In fact, all this working out—the endless treadmill sessions, the yoga classes I rotate through to avoid familiar faces, the weights I habitually lift while zoning out—has given me a hot bod I only dreamed of as a teenager.

I'm practically cut. Lean muscle in my arms, definition in my abs, thighs that don't jiggle anymore when I walk. My ass is an actual shape now instead of just existing.

I look good. I know I look good because men tell me constantly, and I smile and say thank you and ghost them before the third date.

So I check in at the airport counter, sliding my ID across with the kind of casual confidence that still feels like I'm playing dress-up in someone else's life.

I go through security without incident—no beeping, no pat-downs, just a smooth glide through the scanner and a polite nod from the TSA agent who doesn't look at me twice because I'm nobody worth remembering.

I get on the plane, settle into my window seat, buckle in, and let myself disappear into the hum of takeoff while scrolling mindlessly through my phone.

And two hours and five minutes later—after a complimentary ginger ale I didn't finish and a packet of pretzels I ate just to have something to do with my hands— I'm stepping off the jetway into McCarran International Airport, surrounded by the chaotic symphony of slot machines dinging and chiming, people rushing past with roller bags, and that enormous Welcome to Las Vegas sign lit up like a whore on Christmas, glittering, and shameless, and utterly, perfectly alive.

My smile is so big it feels like my face might crack open. I feel reborn before the glow-up has even officially started, before I've set foot in a salon, or touched a poker chip, or done anything except breathe in recycled airport air that somehow smells like possibility.

Modern life is a fucking miracle when you have money.

The taxi pulls up to a porte-cochère that's quieter than the main Strip chaos, bronze-toned and understated in that way expensive things whisper instead of shout. A sign reads *Wynn Tower Suites - Private Entrance* and I feel like I'm sneaking into somewhere I don't belong.

Except I do belong. I paid for this. Well. Caleb paid for this, technically, but the money's in my account now so it counts.

The valet opens my door before I can reach for the handle. "Welcome to the Tower Suites, miss."

I mumble something that might be thank you and step out onto pavement so clean it looks freshly scrubbed. My single carry-on bag feels pathetic suddenly—everyone else arriving here has matched luggage sets and personal assistants.

Inside, the lobby isn't a lobby. It's more like walking into someone's very rich, very tasteful living room. Warm wood paneling, soft amber lighting, a massive floral arrangement on a center table.

No slot machines.

No noise.

Just hushed, rarefied air and the faint scent of something expensive I can't identify.

A woman in an immaculate suit approaches with a smile that's professionally warm without being fake. "Ms. Desmond?"

"Yes," I manage.

"Welcome. I'm Claire, your personal concierge. We have you in a suite on the fifty-eighth floor with Strip views. Your appointments begin in thirty minutes. I booked everything you requested."

I nod like this is normal. Like I do this all the time.

She walks me to a private elevator bank—not the main casino elevators, a completely separate set that requires a key card to access. The doors open immediately because apparently tower suite guests don't wait for anything.

The ride up is silent except for the faint whoosh of expensive machinery. When the doors open on my floor, Claire leads me down a hallway that smells like fresh flowers.

My suite.

My suite.

The door opens and I stop breathing for a second because the space is bigger than my entire old apartment. Floor-to-ceiling windows overlook the Strip—all those flashing lights, and crawling traffic, and chaos spread out below like a glittering infection.

Claire goes through the amenities—minibar, espresso machine, bathroom with the soaking tub, something about turndown service—but I'm not listening. I'm standing at the window, palms pressed against the glass, staring down at thousands of people who have no idea I exist.

No one here knows who I am.

Not ScarletSins. Not the girl who got sold at auction. Not the freak who ran a sex maze in the Caribbean.

Just another anonymous body in a city built for forgetting.

Claire's voice pulls me back. "Your first appointment is in twenty-five minutes, Ms. Desmond. Shall I have them send a car, or would you prefer to walk? The salon is just across the property."

I turn from the window. "I'll walk."

Then I remember the tip. I pull a fifty out of my purse and hand it to her. She doesn't look at it, just smiles at me and backs out.

The salon buzzes with excitement as my stylist—a vision with cascading black hair and a constellation of ear piercings —greets me with a champagne flute and a genuine smile.

"Transform me," I tell her, downing the bubbly like I need courage for what's coming. "Make me look… rich. Make me look… sexy. Hell. Fuck it. Make me look like a goddamned trophy wife."

She laughs. "Darling, by the time I'm done with you, you'll shine like the fucking sun. " She tosses her glossy mane, assessing me with the gleaming eyes of someone who creates magic daily.

I'm seated in the VIP room. Mirrors everywhere. Music pulsing like a heartbeat. Two assistants appear with a platter of chocolate-dipped strawberries. I eat them without reservation.

"Platinum will make those gorgeous eyes pop," the stylist declares, fluffing my hair up as I watch in the mirror.

I drink more champagne, my flute never empty, as she paints my head with bleach. Transforming it into a gleaming sculpture of metallic promise.

I'm seated at a nail station while I process. Gel tips coated in a metallic purple. I've never had long nails in my life. I could look at them for hours, watching them change in the shifting light.

I have the sudden urge to tap things.

The rinse and shampoo massage sends waves of pleasure cascading through my scalp and down my spine. My eyes flutter closed involuntarily as I surrender to sensations so delicious, they border on orgasmic.

Then, I watch—utterly, completely, brazenly transfixed at the magic happening with a blow dryer.

The long, frizzy dirty-blonde hair I walked in with is gone. Replaced by a perfect platinum waterfall that catches every light in the room. Subtle layers framing a face I almost don't recognize.

She was right.

I shine like the fucking sun.

Back in my hotel room, I order room service. A steak that's seared to perfection. A baked potato with everything you can imagine on top. And a gelato that tastes like it came straight from Italy.

This is what money buys.

Not happiness.

Contentment.

I sleep propped up against the floor-to-ceiling window, gazing down at the lights on the Strip, feeling like a platinum-tipped angel instead of a good little slut.

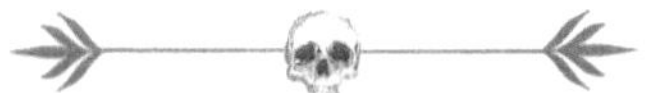

The next morning I have an appointment with an image consultant at ten. I get up extra early to try out the styling products I bought at the salon yesterday. My bathroom counter is a battlefield of unfamiliar bottles and tools, but I'm determined.

I watch a quick tutorial on my phone before attempting to recreate what the stylist did, working the product through my damp hair section by section. I even manage to do a half-good blow out, despite my arms aching halfway through.

My hair doesn't look like it did yesterday—that professional shine and bounce is missing—but it's a thousand times better than it was twenty-four hours ago.

The woman in the mirror actually looks like she gives a damn about herself.

It's startling to see.

I'm pleased with the result. Not ecstatic, not transformed, but pleased.

And realistic.

I know what this is and what it isn't. I'm not some superstar about to walk the red carpet. I'm not deluding myself into thinking a hairstyle will change my life.

Hell, I don't even have a job. Don't want one, either.

My needs are simple, modest.

I just want to feel good about myself. To look in the mirror and not immediately search for flaws. To walk into a room without wanting to disappear.

There has never been a day—not one single day that I can recall—where I ever felt good about myself. Ever.

And that's sad. The kind of sad that sits heavy in your chest when you acknowledge it. The kind of sad that makes me wonder what it would have been like to grow up believing I was worth something.

So when I get to the image consultant's office, this is what I tell her. I'm an everyday girl doing everyday things who wants to feel pretty. Not some Instagram model, not a corporate executive—just someone who deserves to look in the mirror and see something other than disappointment staring back.

After a little interview that narrowed down my style—90's grunge meets Gen Z contradictions—we plan a wardrobe that works for Idaho Falls.

Short summer skirts that hit mid-thigh—lengths I've never dared before—paired with easy, breezy dresses that show off legs I didn't realize I could claim as an asset. Casual crop-top tees in soft cotton, the kind that look effortless but feel intentional. Chunky sandals and boots that work for trails and coffee shops.

Fall outfits with low-cut designer jeans in every shade— dark indigo, faded black, stone-washed grey—all sitting just below my hip bones. The consultant points out my abs in the fitting room mirror, tracing the lines with her finger. I literally didn't even know I had cut abs until that moment.

She pairs them with cropped sweaters in blush pink, warm gray, and cream. Oversized hoodies in black and tan. Soft leggings that actually fit.

For winter she focuses on layering. Long-sleeve cotton tees in black, white, and heather grey that fit close without clinging. Oversized graphic t-shirts to throw on top—vintage band tees, abstract designs, witty slogans that look cool without trying too hard.

I grab some Golden Goose sneakers—the distressed ones that look pre-broken-in. A pair of chunky Balenciagas because everyone has them and honestly they're comfortable as hell. Canvas high-tops in white and another pair in black.

The personal shopper tries to push weatherproof ankle boots and knee-high leather boots "for the Idaho Falls snow," but I just get a pair of chunky lug-sole boots that'll work and don't make me feel like I'm cosplaying someone's mother.

In the coats department, I get a black peacoat that nips in at my waist, a cropped silver puffer jacket, and a long wool coat in charcoal grey that makes me feel like a princess when I spin.

The consultant brings out one statement piece. The little black dress with edge. Exactly what a young woman with brand new long platinum hair needs.

Mid-thigh. Strapless. Plunging neckline.

She pairs it with a vintage leather jacket—oversized, distressed, covered in patches and pins—and chunky combat boots.

The final purchase is activewear. Because let's face it, I spend more time running and at the gym than any reasonable person should. Hiding, obviously. This is how one accidentally gets cut abs without even noticing—anxiety and avoidance sculpting my body while my brain remains a disaster.

But it doesn't have to stay that way. I could actually give a fuck about my workouts now. Set goals and shit. Track progress. Care whether I'm improving or just going through the motions to kill time until I can justify going to bed.

And wouldn't it be nice to look pretty while I did that? To catch my reflection in the gym mirrors and not immediately look away? To feel like I belong on the running trail and in the yoga studio instead of like an imposter hiding among people who actually have their lives together?

Yes. I decide it would. So I buy eight outfits for running, eight outfits for the gym, and eight for yoga. Even though I don't let the laundry pile up anymore, I would like to have one extra for each activity just in case.

I leave the store wearing the black summer mini-dress paired with a vintage band tee knotted at my waist—some obscure metal band I've never even heard of—and the chunky combat boots that make me feel like I could kick someone's ass if needed.

Paired with the platinum hair and a new oversized, black leather Frye bag covered in silver studs, the whole look screams "don't fuck with me" in a way that makes me feel powerful.

I like it.

My final appointment is makeup.

I walk in with mis-matched drug-store products collecting dust at the bottom of my bag—and walk out with Charlotte Tilbury everything.

Lipsticks in shades I'd never have dared try before.

Foundation that actually matches my skin.

Highlighter that catches the light in a way that makes my cheekbones look sculpted rather than sharp with hunger or anxiety.

Brushes so soft they feel like nothing against my skin.

The makeup artist shows me techniques I awkwardly mimic, trying to remember every step.

I don't get room service for my last night in Vegas. I go to dinner. By myself.

Not hidden in a corner booth. Not with a book as a shield. Just me, dressed in new clothes, wearing new makeup, sitting at a table in the center of a crowded restaurant.

The weight of eyes on me still makes my skin crawl. The thought of being judged, found lacking, still tightens my throat. The fear that I'm taking up space I don't deserve still whispers in the back of my mind.

But… it helps.

The new clothes. The makeup. Knowing I look put together, even if I'm falling apart inside.

It also helps when not one, or two, or three—but four men —hit on you. On the way to the restaurant, as I was being seated, the waiter the whole time he served me, his eyes lingering on my face, not my body—and a drunk guy at the craps table while I was walking through the casino on my way back to the elevator.

Men who saw me and thought I was worth approaching, worth talking to, worth pursuing.

It helps.

Not because I need male validation—God knows I've had my fill of the wrong kind of male attention—but because for once, I'm being seen.

Not overlooked.

Not dismissed.

Not avoided.

Seen.

It helps.

CHAPTER 6
CALEB

I'm lurking in the Idaho Falls Regional Airport wearing a navy Adidas tracksuit like some kind of fucking football hooligan, complete with Ray-Bans indoors and a ball cap pulled low.

Ridiculous doesn't begin to cover it.

I look like I'm about to rob a corner shop in Manchester, not wait for a woman at an airport that services maybe six flights a day.

But when Scarletta booked a last-minute ticket to Vegas three days ago, I panicked.

Actually fucking panicked.

Not the controlled assessment of risk and strategic deployment of resources I'm known for. Not the calm calculation that's made me a billionaire and kept me alive through two decades of eliminating human predators.

No.

I lost my fucking mind.

I called in emergency security with the kind of urgency CEOs reserve for hostile takeovers and assassination attempts —not for tracking a twenty-two year old with writer's block on a spontaneous Vegas trip.

Within two hours, I'd deployed three separate tactical teams to follow her every movement. Professional surveillance operators. They had eyes on her from the exact moment she stepped off the plane in Las Vegas.

I could've handled the Vegas situation myself. Should've, probably. Except I don't have access to casino security footage, hotel systems, or the kind of street-level surveillance infrastructure Vegas runs on.

Getting it wouldn't be impossible. Nothing's impossible with enough money and the right leverage. But it would take time I didn't have, and hiring someone local meant trusting strangers with information about her.

Unacceptable.

So I threw obscene amounts of cash at professionals I've vetted personally, sat in my log mansion refreshing their encrypted reports every fifteen minutes like a fucking addict, and hated myself for it.

Now she's back.

Passengers stream through the gate—business travelers in rumpled suits, families with screaming children, college students with backpacks.

And there she is. Exiting the gate pulling a Louie Vuitton carry on. Adjusting a large black leather purse that looks like it contains everything but the secrets of the fucking universe.

Jesus fucking Christ.

I've seen the photos. I know what she did in Vegas—every salon appointment, every boutique, every dollar she finally decided to spend from the accounts I've been filling for six months.

But the photos are bullshit.

Because she's *right here* and my chest just caved in.

The new platinum hair catches the light and I forget how to breathe. That face—those fucking cheekbones I used to trace with my thumb, that mouth I've kissed until she couldn't think—now glossed and pink like she's someone else entirely.

Except she's not someone else.

She's *more* herself.

The woman I always knew was buried under all that fear and self-loathing walks toward me in a black sundress and strappy heels that make her legs look like a fantasy I don't deserve.

She's wearing sunglasses inside too, but they don't make her look like someone trying too hard not to be noticed, they make her look like someone you *should* look at.

Here she comes... I brace for it. The moment she recognizes me. The blow up. The tantrum at my stalking. She's close enough to touch. I don't move. Can't move.

And... she walks right past.

Doesn't even glance my direction.

And why would she?

Why the hell would she give the tracksuit-wearing asshole lurking by the arrivals gate like a fucking stalker a single moment of her time.

Every man in this airport has stopped what he's doing to gape at her.

Like she's an A-list celebrity fresh off the Walk of Fame.

And here I am, frozen like an idiot, watching her disappear toward baggage claim while my heart does something uncomfortable in my chest.

I stand there like a fucking idiot for five seconds too long.

Then I force myself to move—walking toward the exit at a measured pace, not hurrying, not panicking, just another traveler leaving the airport.

Outside, I round the corner of the terminal building and stop.

Press my back against the concrete wall.

Close my eyes.

Breathe.

My heart's pounding like I just sprinted ten miles. Like I'm standing over a corpse with blood on my hands and sirens closing in.

Except there's no threat here. No danger. No reason for my pulse to be hammering against my ribs like it's trying to break through.

It's just *her*.

Walking past me like I don't exist.

Which is exactly what I told her to do, isn't it? *You'll have to come to me.*

I said that. Meant it. Walked away from that alley believing I had the discipline to wait.

And here I am. At her fucking airport. In a tracksuit. Hiding behind a wall because seeing her walk past nearly broke me.

Christ.

I drag a hand down my face, force myself to inventory the situation like I would any other problem requiring tactical assessment.

She didn't recognize me.

The disguise worked.

I followed her to Vegas via surveillance teams, tracked her every movement for three days, and flew here to watch her walk through an airport.

This is not normal behavior.

I don't give a fuck.

I pull myself together and step away from the wall, heading back towards the baggage claim. My steps are quick, almost frantic. I can't afford to miss a single moment—miss what she's doing, who she might be talking to, who might approach her. The thought of someone else catching her attention makes my jaw clench tight enough to hurt.

I force myself to slow down, adopt a casual posture despite the urgency coursing through me. This isn't a board meeting I can dominate with presence alone. This is surveillance, requiring patience and invisibility.

I need to see. Need to know. Need to watch her every move like oxygen.

There are only two baggage claims for the entire airport, so there she is. Standing like she hasn't got a care in the world as suitcases slide down the conveyor.

I freeze, watching a parade of Louis Vuitton bags tumble down the conveyor belt toward Scarletta. She lunges forward with uncharacteristic urgency, her small frame darting between other travelers as she snags one, then another. The third—an oversized monstrosity—eludes her grasp, but then a man's tanned arm reaches past her shoulder to hoist it effortlessly from the belt.

My vision narrows, tunneling onto this unwelcome intrusion. Every muscle in my body tightens as I analyze him —sculpted biceps straining against a fitted shirt, perfect teeth flashing in what he probably thinks is a charming smile. The type who measures his self-worth in protein shakes and bench press maxes.

He's pushing the bag toward her now. Their fingers brush. She's looking up at him, head tilted, lips moving in what appears to be gratitude. The familiarity between them radiates like a physical force, striking me with each second I observe their interaction.

What the hell is happening here?

Do they… do they *know* each other?

The familiarity is unmistakable. They do. Who the hell is this guy? I'm frantically searching my brain, trying to figure it out, when he swings a backpack up on his shoulder.

The logo on the backpack reads Iron River Fitness.

Oh.

Fuck.

The gym owner. Ryan something.

I don't have access to cameras in the gym, they're on a private network with corporate level firewalls. Any time I want eyes on her in there, I've sent in spies. I used to have someone follow her there every day, but her routine is predictable and boring. She blends into the machines. Stays out of the way. Doesn't interact. So these days it's maybe once a week.

Less, actually, now that I think about it.

Did I miss something here?

Has she started a relationship with Ryan what's-his-name?

No. Impossible. She was dating Marty just three days ago.

So this is... nothing. It's nothing. Just two people in an airport...

Wait, are they walking out together? He's pulling two of her suitcases, she's pulling her carry-on and another case, and they're... yeah. They're walking out together!

What the fuck is happening here?

I stalk, careful to stay hidden in the meager crowd. Watching through the glass doors as they step into the August heat together.

Ryan positions her suitcases carefully, then straightens, saying something that makes her laugh. Not a polite laugh. A real one. Her head tilts back, blonde hair catching sunlight, and I can see her shoulders shake.

He's leaning in closer now, gesturing with his hands. Animated. Confident. The kind of casual body language that speaks of familiarity, of comfort.

She's smiling.

Not the nervous, uncertain expression she wore around Marty. Not the blank performance mask she's been wearing for six months while going through the motions of pretending to be normal.

She's genuinely fucking smiling at this man.

My jaw locks tight enough that my teeth ache.

A black Honda pulls up to the curb. Scarletta checks her phone, confirms the license plate. Ryan immediately moves to load her luggage into the trunk—all four pieces, organized efficiently like he's done this before.

Has he done this before?

How many times has he helped her with her bags? How many conversations have they had that I don't know about?

The angle's wrong. I can't read their lips. Can't hear a single fucking word over the traffic noise and distance.

Ryan closes the trunk, walks her to the passenger door. Opens it for her like a gentleman. She turns to say something —probably thank you, probably goodbye—and he responds with what looks like "see you soon."

She gets in.

The door closes.

The Uber pulls away from the curb.

And Ryan stands there watching it drive away, hands in his pockets, wearing a smile like he just won something.

I'm not sure how much time passes before I actually snap out of the fugue state watching Scarletta respond to actual flirting from a non-beta male put me in, but the airport pick-up lanes are quieter now.

I make my way to my Jeep, get in, start it up… sit there.

She's not going to come to me.

A woman doesn't drop everything to book a glow-up trip to Vegas because she's looking to go backwards.

A woman does that when she's put the past behind her.

I pull out of the airport and begin the drive back to Jackson. I need to think this through and I don't have somewhere to properly do that in Idaho Falls.

I don't put on tunes.

Don't even register the rolling farmlands and small-town charm in Victor. Those picturesque stretches of rural Idaho where red barns dot green fields and weathered fences line the road like something out of a postcard.

Don't look at the beautiful mountain scenery through Teton Pass as I navigate the tight switchbacks—the towering peaks and dramatic ridge lines that usually pull my attention, the kind of raw wilderness that normally grounds me when everything else feels chaotic.

Don't do anything but think as I make the two-hour drive back to my log mansion in the woods.

My mind is a closed loop playing the same thirty-second clip on repeat: Ryan's easy conversation. Her laugh. The way she leaned into him like they were friends, like she'd done it a hundred times before.

What the fuck is happening here?

Later, back at home, I'm pacing the office. Phone in hand, mind twisting, thoughts spiraling…

I'm losing her.

I gave her space. Clean break. I was very careful with my voyeurism. Public places. Cornerstone's hacked security, the Greenbelt trail cams, Iron River's front door from the public camera across the street.

She took the cameras down in her old apartment. She deleted my key logger hack on her old laptop.

I respected her decision. I pulled back. I didn't even try to infiltrate her new place downtown. I didn't even try to hack her wi-fi and insert a new key logger.

I backed the fuck off.

I gave her *space*.

That was the mistake.

I have no idea what she does in that new apartment. I didn't keep a good eye on the gym and what she's been doing in there.

Maybe Ryan has been flirting with her for months—subtle compliments, lingering eye contact across the room, that practiced charm he probably deploys without thinking.

Maybe this whole time, while I was carefully curating my distance, he was slowly circling closer.

Or, more likely, he never noticed her at all.

And then… one day… he's in the airport—why? Why was he there? I'll find out, but doesn't really matter. He was. At the baggage claim with nothing but a backpack. And they see each other.

She's transformed.

From mousy introvert to stunning Instagram fantasy.

He's transfixed, recovers quickly enough to pull the heaviest suitcase from the conveyor, small talk.

Wow, look at you!

Yeah, I look hot, don't I? Do you wanna fuck me now?

Right now, my good little slut. Right the fuck now. Bend over this suitcase, pull your dress up, let me spread those perfect cheeks apart and see that glistening pussy waiting for me.

I'm absolutely soaking for you, Ryan. Please, I need you inside me! Fuck me right here against the baggage claim! Don't hold back —I want it rough!

I scoff.

Ridiculous. New hair doesn't change an entire personality.

Also, I should definitely not quit my day job. That pathetic little fantasy I just conjured was… frankly embarrassing.

I'm absolutely soaking for you, Ryan?

Scarletta wouldn't say that. She'd beg for his cock., though.

Please, please fuck me.

That's more her style. She'd probably call him Master.

Give me that cock, Master.

I can picture that easy enough. I'm the fucking one who trained her to say those words out loud instead of locking them up in a story, after all.

I keep spiraling.

Ryan would pin her against his truck in the airport parking garage. Scarletta would melt against him, her new nails scratching down his back, those purple-tipped fingers digging into his shoulders.

He'd hike up that black sundress, discover she's wearing nothing underneath and he'd finger her, right there in public.

She'd moan his name. Beg him to fuck her.

Please, Ryan. I need you. I need your cock inside me.

He'd turn her around, bend her over the hood of his truck, and slide into her dripping wet pussy in one brutal thrust.

She'd gasp, arch her back, push her ass against him for more.

Harder. Please. Fuck me harder.

And Ryan would oblige, wouldn't he? Big strong gym owner, all that testosterone and athletic stamina. He'd pound into her like she was his personal fuck toy, one hand fisted in her new platinum hair, the other gripping her hip hard enough to bruise.

She'd come screaming his name.

Then he'd pull out, flip her around, make her kneel, and shove his cock down her throat until she choked on it, tears streaming down her face, mascara running—

I stop pacing.

My cock is rock hard.

I'm standing in the middle of my office, imagining another man fucking the woman I'm obsessed with, and I'm *aroused*.

What the fuck is wrong with me?

I drag a hand through my hair, forcing myself to breathe through the arousal, to think rationally about what's happening to me.

Nothing. There's nothing wrong with me. I've done this before—stood in the control room and watched the attendants work her body with their skilled, indifferent hands, watched her writhe and beg and come apart for them while I stroked myself through my pants.

I've reviewed those recordings a dozen times since, jerked off to the memory of her spread out like an offering, three sets of hands mapping every inch of her skin while she trembled and moaned. I've replayed the moment she shattered, the way she screamed and arched off that table, and I've come so hard I saw stars.

This is just another iteration of the same theme. Just a voyeuristic fantasy. Nothing more than that. Completely meaningless in the grand scheme of things.

Probably not… it's almost certainly a sickness. Some deep-rooted perversion I inherited from my father, coded into my DNA like a genetic curse I can't escape.

I'm aroused by sick things. Depraved scenarios that would make most men recoil in disgust. The darker the fantasy, the harder I get—that's always been my burden, my shame, the proof that my mother was right when she looked at me with those hollow eyes and said *you're just like him* before stepping off that balcony.

That's why Scarletta hates me now. Why she ran. Why she rebuilt herself into someone who dates yoga instructors and gym owners, men with uncomplicated desires and healthy relationships with sex.

She's not scared of me. I don't think that's it. Fear would be simpler—I could work with fear, negotiate around it, prove myself safe despite the darkness. But what I saw in her eyes during those final moments on the island wasn't terror.

It was revulsion.

I just… repulse her. The real me, the one she glimpsed when I showed her what I'm truly capable of, what I truly *want*—she finds me disgusting. And maybe she's right. Maybe that's the only sane response to a man like me.

She wants men like this Ryan now—gym owners with uncomplicated desires and straightforward lives.

Men who fuck in bright bedrooms with the lights on, who think "adventurous" means trying a new position or maybe some light hair-pulling.

Men whose darkness extends to watching rough porn

occasionally, not to the intricate psychological labyrinths I construct in my mind.

Men who have big cocks and know how to use them competently, satisfactorily, without needing the complex power dynamics that fuel my every sexual thought.

Men whose kink tolerance peaks at fuzzy handcuffs from a novelty shop, not canes meant to scar.

Normal men. Healthy men. Men who don't carry their father's violence in their blood like a hereditary disease.

I'm not normal and I'm not going to apologize for it.

Not to Scarletta, not to the world, not even to the conscience that occasionally surfaces in the small hours before dawn.

The world needs men like me. Men who operate in the shadows where polite society refuses to look. Men who understand that true evil—the kind that traffics children, that destroys innocence for profit, that hides behind philanthropy and political connections—that kind of evil doesn't respond to strongly worded condemnations or legal proceedings that take years while more victims accumulate.

Men who are willing to become monsters to hunt monsters are necessary.

Men who keep the truly evil, the truly horrific predators like Volk in check when the systems designed to stop them fail over, and over, and over again, essential.

I'm practically a fucking superhero, if you think about it objectively. Dexter with better taste and a higher body count of people who actually deserved it.

What the world doesn't need... is another fucking gym owner.

I could make it look like an accident.

Gyms are dangerous places. Heavy equipment, faulty cables, catastrophic mechanical failures that crush windpipes or snap spines.

A bench press bar to the throat. Quick. Efficient. Tragic

gym accident, nobody's fault, terrible loss for the fitness community.

But that's not satisfying.

That doesn't account for him touching what's mine. Loading her luggage like some helpful fucking Boy Scout. Making her laugh—genuine laughter I haven't heard in months, maybe ever. Opening her door like a gentleman when he has no idea what she really needs, what she truly craves.

He doesn't deserve quick.

I could take my time instead.

I'd subdue him—chloroform, taser, doesn't matter. Wake up restrained in my barn. Confused, terrified, asking why the fuck I'm doing this.

Because you touched something that belongs to me.

Simple. Honest. He'd understand then, in those final hours.

I've never killed anyone in my barn before. Never needed to. The cabin's always been my personal space—retreat, refuge, the place I disappear to between jobs. The barn's just storage. Firewood. The industrial furnace I use for burning evidence from kills that happen elsewhere.

But it's got that walk-in freezer.

Previous owners were hunters. Elk, moose, whatever the fuck. Built the freezer custom, restaurant-grade cooling, thick insulation, heavy steel door with a manual lock from the outside.

Perfect for hanging a carcass while it ages.

Perfect for keeping a man alive while you work on him slowly.

I'm rock-hard, pulse pounding in my temples, cock straining painfully against my zipper. I drop into my chair and shove the waistband of my pants down roughly, freeing my erection. It springs up, already leaking. I wrap my fist around myself and start stroking—fast, rough, no finesse—while the images keep coming.

Ryan's blood spreading across frozen concrete. Steam rising from the spreading pool. His body convulsing as shock sets in, his pathetic attempts to beg through the gag becoming weaker, more desperate.

I'd take my time after that. Hours. Maybe days if I kept him conscious enough.

Peel his skin off in strips. Start with the fingers—those hands that touched her luggage, that opened her car door like he had any fucking right.

My hand moves faster now, rougher, punishing. I'm gripping myself so tight it almost hurts, but I don't ease up.

The images come quicker now, sharper.

Ryan screaming as I work the knife under his fingernails. Ryan thrashing when I remove his eyes with a melon baller. Ryan whimpering as I break every bone in his hands with a ball-peen hammer, methodical, thorough, crushing each knuckle individually.

I'd make art of his suffering.

Document every stage. Photographs. Video. Send them to Scarletta afterward so she understands what happens when other men think they can have her.

This is what I do to people who touch what's mine.

I imagine Ryan's final moments. Hypothermic, mutilated, barely conscious. I'd stand over him and jerk off, just like I did with Volk. Come all over his ruined face while he dies watching me.

The orgasm hits like a physical blow. I grunt, hips jerking up as I spill all over my hand, my shirt, my desk. Thick ropes of come painting my stomach while the fantasy plays out its brutal conclusion behind my closed eyes.

I keep stroking through the aftershocks, milking every drop while I imagine Scarletta finding out what I've done.

The horror in her eyes. The knowledge that I'd kill anyone who tried to take her from me.

Finally spent, I slump back in my chair, cock still twitching, come cooling on my skin.

I don't feel shame.

I don't feel remorse.

I feel *satisfied*.

This is who I am. What I am. A man who gets hard imagining elaborate torture scenarios. A man who comes thinking about murder, and mutilation, and making people suffer for the crime of existing near what belongs to him.

I'm not going to apologize for it.

I'm not going to change, either.

This.

Is who.

I am.

CHAPTER 7
SCARLETTA

My new closet is *insane*.

Like, objectively ridiculous for someone who spent most of her adult life living in blanket forts and wearing her dead dad's hoodie for a week straight without showering.

But here I am, standing in front of it like I'm admiring art or something, staring at all my Vegas purchases hanging in perfect color-coordinated rows. The image consultant taught me that—organize by color family, then by occasion. Casual to formal. Light to dark.

I actually *did* it when I got home.

Unpacked everything immediately instead of leaving the suitcases on the floor for three weeks like I normally would. Hung every dress. Folded every shirt. Arranged my new shoes on the bottom rack like I'm some kind of functioning adult who has their shit together.

The Golden Goose sneakers next to the Balenciagas. Combat boots lined up with the heeled booties. My statement LBD hanging next to the vintage leather jacket like they're a power couple.

It's giving *girl who plans outfits the night before* energy.

It's giving *person who owns a lint roller and uses it* vibes.

Honestly? It's giving *not me at all*.

But I kind of... love it?

I reach out and touch the sleeve of the leather jacket. A statement piece I paid real money for instead of scrolling past longingly on Pinterest before closing the tab and eating Lucky Charms standing over the sink.

My platinum hair catches in the closet's LED strip lighting and I barely recognize my own reflection in the full-length mirror.

Trophy wife hair. Designer clothes. Abs I never noticed before.

Who the *fuck* am I?

I stare at my reflection and the answer slams into me with unexpected force.

I'm Scarletta fucking Desmond.

ScarletSins.

That's who I am. That's who I've always been, underneath all the self-sabotage, and unwashed hoodies, and three-day-old coffee mugs.

This closet—this whole apartment, this whole *life*—it proves it. This is what the writer looks like when she stops hiding. When she stops performing poverty and dysfunction like they're personality traits.

I'm... cool.

The thought is so foreign it almost makes me laugh. But it's true, isn't it? I'm cool now. I have my shit together. I wake up at 5 AM and go for runs and drink lattes I don't finish because I can afford to waste six dollars on a beverage I'm using as a prop.

But even as I'm standing here having this moment of self-actualization—this *look at me being a whole-ass person* epiphany—something else crashes into my brain.

A character flaw. A major one.

The old apartment.

I just... walked away from it. Packed two suitcases and left everything else sitting there like a crime scene I couldn't bear to process.

All of it still *there*, waiting. Like some kind of horrible museum exhibit of who I used to be.

The Girl Who Gave Up: A Retrospective.

I left it because... what? Some fucked-up part of me thought maybe I'd go back one day? That I'd need an escape hatch back into dysfunction if this whole "being okay" thing didn't work out?

Why the fuck would I *ever* go back?

I need to get rid of it. All of it. Every last piece of that life I've been dragging around like dead weight.

Like, right now. Tonight. This minute.

I grab my laptop and flip it open with more force than necessary. The screen glows to life and I navigate to Google with shaking hands.

Junk removal Idaho Falls.

A dozen results appear and I click the first one with a functioning website. There's an online booking form and I fill it out rapid-fire, barely reading the questions.

Address. Date. Time. Special instructions.

Take everything. I don't care where it goes. Just get it out.

I hit submit before I can second-guess myself.

It's late and I'm tired, so I'm putting this day to bed. But tomorrow I'm going over there to grab the two things I still want and burn the past down so I can never crawl back into it again.

Holy *shit*. I have a goal.

The realization makes me pause, laptop still warm on my thighs, cursor blinking on the confirmation screen.

I have a *goal*. An actual, concrete, "I'm going to do this thing tomorrow" goal that isn't just "survive" or "try not to implode."

A smile tugs at the corner of my mouth. Small at first, then wider.

After six months of aimless wandering and depression, the new me is... here.

I'm *here*.

I'm *her*.

The girl in the mirror with the platinum hair, and the statement pieces, and the abs she didn't know she had.

The girl who books junk removal at ten PM on a weeknight and doesn't spiral about it for three days first.

The girl who's done performing poverty like it's a personality.

I'm fucking *here*.

The next day I do my regular run routine, but skip the coffee shop. Instead I drive over to my old apartment.

When I open the door, it smells stale. Like old laundry—which, fair. There are piles of it everywhere.

And I'm... embarrassed.

Absolutely fucking mortified.

I close the door behind me and walk into the small living space. How did I get to be such a slob?

But it's not really a mystery, is it? And the answer comes right out of my mouth before I can stop it. "You were depressed, Scarletta. For probably—hell, your whole damn life."

The words hang there in the stale air of the apartment.

It's true.

I've been depressed for so long—years and years of it, this low-grade fog that settled over everything—that it took me six full months of structured routines and forced normalcy to even begin to recognize what happiness might look like. What it might feel like if I ever let myself reach for it.

But now... I know what this place really was.

It wasn't a home. It wasn't even a proper living space. This cramped, cluttered studio with its piles of unwashed clothes, and dishes crusted in the sink, and that futon I never bothered to make—it was a holding cell. A place I retreated to when the world got too loud, too demanding, too *real*.

It was where I came to disappear.

This apartment was my desperate, failing attempt to hold on to whatever threads of sanity I had left. To maintain some illusion that I was a functional adult with a life, even as I let everything—my body, my space, my finances, my relationships—rot around me.

And I want it to go away. I want this entire chapter of my existence erased.

I want to never think about the girl who lived here again.

But I'm not leaving my laptop behind. There are forty-seven complete stories saved in its hard drive. Plus another dozen I never finished. Stories I poured myself into during the worst nights, when writing was the only thing that kept me tethered to something resembling purpose.

Those stories were written by a mentally ill woman who lived in darkness and filth and couldn't see a way out. But they're still mine. They still matter. The words themselves—the characters, the scenes, the twisted beautiful connections I built between broken people—those are real, even if the person who wrote them was barely holding on.

I'm taking them with me. They get to survive, even if she doesn't.

I crawl inside the glamping tent and there it is, right in the center of the space. The lid is open, screen dark and lifeless after months of neglect, battery long since drained. But it's positioned deliberately, waiting for me to find it.

I lie back on the soft rug that came with the tent and stare up at the canopy of fairy lights strung overhead. They're dead too, just dim bulbs hanging limp against white fabric.

But I can see where Caleb strung them, how carefully he arranged them to create the illusion of stars. The same way he arranged everything else in this bizarre, thoughtful, completely unhinged gesture.

He saw me—actually saw me, beneath the performance and the desperate scrambling for normalcy.

And yes, the methods were... unconventional doesn't even begin to cover it. He orchestrated a fake auction where I thought I was selling myself to the highest bidder.

He made me come so hard I blacked out, over and over until I forgot my own name.

He sent me into that goddamn maze—my own twisted creation made flesh—where masked men were supposed to hunt me through bamboo corridors while his voice guided me deeper into manufactured terror.

I still don't fully understand what happened that day. Who that Russian man was or why he was there.

It's all very fucked up.

Top to bottom insane.

Certifiably unhinged by any reasonable metric.

But... if you read between the lines and see the subtext underneath... it makes sense.

He didn't actually buy me. The auction was theater, carefully staged to make me feel something—anything—again.

The hunt wasn't real either. That maze was a retelling of something I loved dearly, but had to throw away because it broke all the rules and filled me with shame.

He didn't call me his good little slut because he thinks I'm some disposable fucktoy. He said it because he knew—somehow knew—that I needed someone to see the darkness I'd been hiding and call it beautiful instead of broken.

He did all that batshit crazy stuff because he... *believed in me.*

The man is sick. Absolutely fucked in the head to a degree that probably requires institutionalization and medication.

But he *saw* me.

He replaced my pathetic blanket fort, a literal representation of my own deteriorating mental health, with a luxury glamping tent.

He put up an actual Christmas tree and filled it with ornaments I chose and desperately wanted, but could never afford.

He left cookies and milk out for Santa, then took a bite and sip so I'd understand exactly what this was.

Not a cage.

Not a trap.

A *gift*.

And that's all before he started filling bank accounts with endless millions of dollars. So many fucking dollars, I'm probably going to prison for tax evasion because I just keep ignoring it.

I came here for two things and now it's time to go.

I push the laptop out of the tent as I scramble out, then go over to the little tree—completely brown and dead—and pick off all the ornaments, shoving them into my massive purse.

Then I take one last look around before leaving, closing the door behind me.

It's over.

Whatever Caleb was to me, it's done. I've moved on.

But the man deserves credit where credit is due.

Without him…

I can't even think it, but I *must*.

Without him… I'd probably be dead.

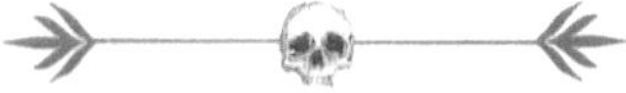

I dump everything on my kitchen counter—laptop, dead ornaments, the weight of my entire former existence—and head straight for my bedroom.

I strip out of my sundress and dig through the activewear section until I find the black leggings with the mesh cutouts running down the sides and a matching sports bra that actually fits properly. There's a cropped hoodie too—charcoal gray, expensive fabric that moves like water.

In the mirror, I look... different.

Not just the platinum hair or the new clothes.

Something about my posture has changed. My shoulders don't curl inward anymore. I'm not trying to disappear into myself.

I grab my new gym bag, fill it with the essentials, then I head out.

Downtown Idaho Falls isn't exactly bustling, but the afternoon sunlight makes everything feel lighter somehow. People pass me on the sidewalk and I don't immediately catalog all the ways they're judging me.

Some of them aren't even looking at me.

The ones who are... they're not looking at me like I'm something broken they need to avoid.

I feel satisfied. Complete, almost.

Like I'm exactly where I'm supposed to be, doing exactly what I should be doing, instead of hiding in a blanket fort pretending the world doesn't exist.

And maybe—just maybe—I'm thinking about Ryan.

Not in the usual way. Not the desperate, frantic fantasizing that used to consume me about fictional men doing terrible things.

Just... Ryan.

How he smiled at the airport when he saw my new hair. *"Holy shit, Scarletta. You look amazing."*

How he insisted on helping me with my suitcases even though I told him I could manage.

How he opened the Uber door and told me *"See you soon,"* like he actually meant it.

I was genuinely flattered that he even *noticed* me.

I'd noticed *him*, obviously. You can't miss Ryan at Iron River Fitness. His office sits elevated in the center of the gym floor like some kind of glass fishbowl, and he's always up there—watching his clientele with this benevolent intensity, like he actually cares whether people hit their goals.

He's objectively gorgeous. Tall, broad-shouldered, perfectly sculpted in that way that suggests he actually lives the lifestyle he sells. His body is covered in bird tattoos—and I mean *covered*. Sleeves that disappear under his shirt, ink crawling up his neck, vanishing beneath his collar.

They're not random flash pieces scattered across his skin. They're intricate, custom work. Each bird is different—ravens, swallows, hawks—rendered in this incredible detail that suggests hours in the chair and serious money spent.

Beautiful doesn't quite cover it. They're art. The kind of tattoos that tell a story, even if I don't know what that story is yet.

Completely out of my league.

That's where my attention stopped. Because why torture myself imagining scenarios where someone like Ryan would want someone like me?

Except...

Maybe I'm not out of his league anymore.

Maybe—and this feels dangerous to even think—maybe I'm exactly his type.

He was certainly friendly at the airport.

Really friendly.

I round the corner and Iron River Fitness comes into view, all glass and chrome, and the promise of people who've figured out how to exist in their bodies without hating themselves.

My heart does this stupid flutter thing.

Because Ryan might be in there.

And for the first time in my entire goddamn life, I'm not immediately constructing elaborate reasons why someone wouldn't want me.

I push through the glass doors and immediately scan the

gym floor. Looking for Ryan. Hating myself a little that I'm looking for Ryan.

Because that's what I do, right? Fixate on men who—

"Scarletta!"

And there he is. Walking toward me with that easy confidence, wearing a fitted black shirt that does absolutely nothing to hide the fact that he's built like some kind of Greek statue.

My brain short-circuits. "Hey," I manage, and I sound almost normal. Almost.

"I was starting to worry you weren't gonna show up today." He stops in front of me, close enough that I have to tilt my head back slightly to maintain eye contact. "You're usually here by now."

He's been *thinking* about me.

He knows my schedule.

Heat floods my face and I pray the gym lighting hides how hard I'm blushing.

"I had some business to attend to," I say, forcing my voice to stay steady. "Old life stuff. But I wouldn't miss my daily workout for anything."

Lie.

Except... maybe it's not?

I *have* been coming here every day. Not because I care about fitness goals, or sculpting my body, or any of that motivational poster bullshit.

But because it kills time. Because it's something to do that isn't sitting in my apartment spiraling.

Ryan's gaze sweeps over me—not in a creepy way. Just... appreciative. Professional but warm.

He meets my eyes again and there's something in his expression that makes my stomach flip.

"Want some help with your workout today?" he asks.

"No." The word comes out automatically, defensive. "I

mean, I'm good. I just do the treadmill and stairclimber anyway, so..."

God, I hate myself.

Why did I say it like that? Like I'm apologizing for taking up space? Like I need to justify my boring routine to him?

But Ryan doesn't look put off. If anything, his smile widens.

"How about I give you a new personal fitness plan?" He leans against the counter, casual, easy. "On the house. Your body already looks amazing, Scarletta—seriously, whatever you've been doing is working—but if you'd like to actually *sculpt* it? I'm the guy. I can help."

My mouth goes dry.

Your body already looks amazing.

He thinks my body looks amazing.

Ryan—gorgeous, successful, completely-out-of-my-league Ryan—thinks *I* look amazing.

I should say something.

Anything.

Instead I'm just standing here like an idiot, staring at him, my new metallic purple nails digging into the strap of my gym bag.

"Um... OK." OK? That's it? That's the extent of my game? For fuck's sake, Scarletta, level the fuck up!

"I mean, yes. Obviously—" I slowly lower my eyes, then raise them back up, "—you know what you're doing."

He smiles, then laughs. "Are you dangerous, Scarletta?"

"What?" I giggle.

"That look. Wow. You just checked me the fuck out."

"So? Did you hate it?"

"Not at all, button. I'm diggin' it hard."

"Button?" I snort.

"Yeah." He pauses, smiling all the way up to his gleaming eyes. "You're like... cute as a fuckin' button."

"Oh, my god."

"I'm lame, right?"

"Well… yeah. But…" I let out a breath. We're flirting. And I love it. "Totally lame. Please don't stop."

His smile lingers a few moments too long. Like he's really thinking about this interaction. "So… let's go," he says, and there's something different in his voice now—lower, rougher around the edges.

He steps a little closer, not crowding me but close enough that I can smell whatever clean, woodsy scent he's wearing.

"I'll show you exactly how to turn your already amazing body into something so goddamn fuckable that every single man within a two-hundred-mile radius will be lining up, practically begging for the chance to take you out."

My brain short-circuits.

Fuckable.

He just said *fuckable.*

To my face.

Like it's a completely normal thing to say to someone you're training.

My pulse is hammering so hard I'm pretty sure he can see it in my throat. My face is burning. Every nerve ending in my body just woke up at once, screaming.

I open my mouth. Close it. Open it again.

Nothing comes out.

Ryan's watching me with that same easy confidence, like he didn't just detonate a bomb in the middle of my carefully maintained composure. Like he knows *exactly* what that word did to me—and he's enjoying it.

Then he turns and heads toward the machines—casual, confident, like he didn't just rearrange every single thought in my brain.

While I stay rooted in place.

Mouth open.

Heart pounding.

The word *fuckable* looping on repeat in my head like some kind of filthy mantra I can't shut off.

He wants me.

The realization crashes through me. Hot, and disorienting, and impossibly real.

He actually wants me.

Not hypothetically. Not in some vague, distant, maybe-someday sense.

He wants *me*. Right now. Enough to say it out loud. Enough to use a word like that and watch what it does to me.

My legs feel shaky. My skin feels too tight. Everything inside me is vibrating at a frequency I don't recognize.

I force myself to move. One foot in front of the other.

Hurrying to catch up.

Ready to see exactly where this goes.

CHAPTER 8
CALEB

I'm starting to wonder if I might be obsessed. Not in the casual way I normally am, but… clinical definition.

Because here I am, sitting in a black Tahoe across the street from Iron River Fitness, with enough surveillance equipment to make me look like a Mission Impossible cliche.

The drink-holders are littered with empty coffee cups—three of them, all from different days because apparently I've made this parking spot my second office. In addition to my custom security setup on the dash, there's a laptop balanced on the passenger seat, feeds cycling through every angle I've managed to hack into.

Legal? Absolutely not.

Necessary? Apparently fucking so, because I can't seem to stop myself.

Your assignment, should you choose to accept it, is to determine if your good little slut is actually… not yours at all.

The leather steering wheel creaks under my grip. I force myself to loosen my fingers, to breathe. This is what passes for restraint these days—not breaking inanimate objects while I watch her gym from across the street like some kind of deranged stalker.

Which, let's be honest, is exactly what I am. I've crossed so many lines I can't even see them in the rearview mirror anymore.

It's been nine days since I gave her my card with explicit instructions to find me when she's ready. To contact me. To give me some indication that what happened between us wasn't just a fever dream I manufactured in my own twisted mind.

Three of those days count as travel days since she went to Vegas for her little glow-up.

But actually, the third day doesn't really count as a travel day anymore because Ryan fucking Adamson bumped in to her at the baggage claim.

What if that was planned?

No I can't even consider that.

Why Caleb? It's an honest question. You have no idea what's been happening inside Iron River Fitness. You have no cameras in there. Not a single fucking one.

The point is, two days out of nine.

Two full days she was, for certain, not thinking about Ryan Adamson because she was in Vegas getting new hair, and new nails, and new clothes, and new makeup. A complete transformation. A reinvention.

Trying to forget me.

Trying to scrub away every trace of what happened in the maze. Trying to wash the blood off her hands with platinum blonde dye and Charlotte Tilbury foundation. Trying to bury the memory of my cock spewing long ropes of come all over a corpse.

Trying to put her past behind her—to put *me* behind her.

That's what women do when they break up with a man, isn't it? They reinvent themselves. They emerge from the cocoon as someone new, someone better, someone who never would have done those things in the first place.

They start over. Shiny, and new, and utterly unrecognizable.

Which is bad enough on its own—especially since she hasn't taken a single fucking opportunity to call me. To reach out. To acknowledge my existence. Does she have any concept, any remote understanding, of how many women would literally kill to have my card pressed into their palm with a no-strings offer to come find me whenever they wanted?

Not that I'd ever bring one of those corporate vultures back to my cabin—Christ, no. This is a hard line in the sand for me, drawn in permanent fucking marker. No professional women. Not the lawyers, not the executives, not the consultants who circle me at networking events like sharks scenting blood in the water.

They're catty, and ruthless, and emotional in all the wrong ways—three traits that aren't so much dangerous as they are utterly psychotic. The kind of psychotic that ends with restraining orders, leaked tabloid stories, and property damage.

The point is—because apparently I need to keep circling back to 'the point'—the card itself was never meant to be casual. It wasn't some throwaway business gesture, some LinkedIn connection request made flesh.

That little rectangle of embossed cardstock with my private number and address, for fucks sake, represented something I don't offer. Something I've spent the better part of a decade *not* offering, to anyone, under any circumstances.

It was an admission. A crack in the armor. A fucking *invitation* written in a language I don't speak with anyone else, to come out to my secret Batcave where I go to unwind after balancing the scales and dispose of evidence.

And what did she do with it?

She tossed it in whatever mental garbage bin holds all the other mistakes she's trying to erase from her life. Shoved it into that desktop folder called 'Do not Open' right alongside being raped by Derek and stories that cross all the lines.

She probably really has been lusting over Ryan all these months. Building him up in her head as the safe alternative, the normal choice, which in that case means...

I sigh and just allow myself to think it. To sit with the discomfort of the thought like pressing on a bruise to confirm it still hurts.

Go ahead, Caleb. Say the words. If not out loud, at least in the privacy of your own goddamn head.

She really has moved on.

The sight of me coming all over a dead body was her limit. Her actual, genuine, non-negotiable hard limit.

I'm her hard limit.

Should I feel good about this? Like some perverse achievement unlocked? *Hey, congratulations, you're so fundamentally fucked up that you're the actual hard limit for the woman who wrote Call of the Labyrinth—a book where every single scene is a rape fantasy minus the fantasy part, where the heroine gets hunted, and captured, and violated three separate times by literal animals before accepting captivity as the better option.*

The descriptions of their cocks included the word 'fur'.

Fur, for fucks sake.

The woman who dreamed *that* up, who lived inside that narrative for months while writing it, looked at me and thought: *Nope. This is too much. He is too much.*

I sigh, and the sound that comes out is something closer to defeat than I've allowed myself in years.

Why am I doing this?

That's the actual question, isn't it? Not *what* I'm doing—because what I'm doing is abundantly fucking clear. I'm sitting in a vehicle across from a gym, tracking a woman who doesn't want to be tracked, inserting myself into her life in increasingly unhinged ways while pretending I'm respecting her boundaries.

The *why* is the part I keep avoiding.

Why Idaho Falls? Why this parking spot? Why am I watching Iron River Fitness like it holds answers I don't want to hear?

Why did I give her the card in the first place?

Why does the thought of her with Ryan Adamson—a perfectly decent man who owns a gym and probably has a golden retriever and uses phrases like "let's grab coffee sometime"—make me want to burn the entire building to the ground?

I could be anywhere. I have three homes, multiple offshore accounts, enough resources to disappear completely if I wanted. I run a billion-dollar investment firm from my laptop. I coordinate international operations for The Scales without ever leaving Jackson Hole.

I don't *need* to be here.

But I drove two hours to sit in this parking lot for the third time this week, waiting for a glimpse of platinum blonde hair and combat boots.

Waiting for her.

My throat tightens around something I don't have a name for.

Or rather—I do have a name for it. I just don't want to say it. Don't want to acknowledge what it means, what it implies about the carefully constructed architecture of my entire fucking life.

Because if I say it, it becomes real.

If I say it, then everything I've told myself about control, and ownership, and possession gets reframed into something infinitely more dangerous.

Possession I understand. Obsession I can justify. Even the stalking, and surveillance, and orchestrated manipulation—I can rationalize all of it through the lens of dominance and submission. Of giving her what she wrote about wanting, of being exactly the monster she needed.

But this?

This sitting in parking lots and tracking her movements and feeling my chest constrict when she flirts with another man?

This isn't dominance. This is something else entirely.

I grip the steering wheel again, forcing the words into existence inside my own head where no one else can hear them.

I might actually love her.

The admission sits there like a grenade with the pin pulled.

Not obsession dressed up as devotion. Not possession masquerading as protection.

Actual love. The kind that makes you rearrange your entire existence around someone else's orbit. The kind that turns you into a version of yourself you don't recognize—softer in some ways, more dangerous in others.

The kind that makes you give someone a card with your private number and Batcave address and then wait, like an idiot, for them to use it.

I force myself to take a deep breath.

Then another.

Then I do something so fucking pathetic I can barely stand myself.

I open a new document on my laptop and title it: Scarletta Desmond - Assessment.

Like I'm preparing a quarterly earnings report. Like she's a potential acquisition target that requires due diligence.

Like I'm a teenage girl with a fucking diary.

I start typing.

CONS.

My fingers hover over the keys for a moment before I commit.

She's a slob. Six months of surveillance footage doesn't lie. Dishes piled in the sink for weeks. Laundry mountains that probably qualified as biohazards. The blanket fort wasn't charming—it was depression architecture. She lived like someone who'd given up on herself completely.

She has no ambition. Forty-seven complete stories posted anonymously online for free. Not a single one submitted to an agent or publisher. Brilliant work rotting in digital obscurity because she's too terrified of rejection to even try. She'd rather starve than risk someone telling her she's not good enough.

She's financially incompetent. Four months behind on rent. Maxed credit cards. Student loans in default.

She ghosts people. Clients. Yoga instructors. Every man she's dated in the last six months. The second anything requires emotional vulnerability or follow-through, she vanishes. Runs away. Disappears like she never existed in the first place.

She lies to herself constantly. Attends support groups she doesn't belong to. Performs normalcy for strangers. Pretends she wants vanilla relationships with nice guys when her entire creative output is rape fantasies and psychological torture. She's a walking contradiction who refuses to admit what she actually needs.

She's a coward. Wrote Call of the Labyrinth and never published it. Signed up for the auction and then tried to pretend she didn't want it. Entered the maze and then ran away when I gave her exactly what she asked for.

I stop typing.

My jaw aches from clenching.

She ran away when you murdered someone in front of her, you absolute psychopath.

I delete that last line about the maze. That one's not fair. That one's on me.

I stare at the list.

Everything I wrote is true. Objectively, factually accurate.

She's a mess. A beautiful, brilliant, infuriating fucking mess.

And I'm sitting in a parking lot across from a gym making

notes about her flaws like some kind of deranged consultant trying to talk himself out of a merger.

The problem is… I don't want to admit this but I have to. The problem is… I don't see a way forward without her.

My list grows, but these goes under the heading, Things I Can't Control Anymore.

Can't focus worth shit. I used to deliver surgical presentations at board meetings. Now I'm checking my phone every thirty seconds like some lovesick teenager waiting for a text that never comes.

Sleep's fucked. I used to run on five hours, sharp as a blade. Now I'm lucky if I get three, and those are full of her face, her voice, her new platinum fucking hair.

Surveillance has become my second job. I've got tactical teams deployed like she's a head of state. Three different shifts. Round-the-clock coverage. This is not normal behavior, even for me.

Haven't balanced the scales in months. Volk broke me. *No, Caleb. Scarletta watching you kill him and then rejecting you, broke you.*

How did this happen?

How?

How did I get here?

I scoff out loud, that's how ridiculous this question is.

Scarletta put me here.

I lean back in the driver's seat, letting my head hit the headrest.

Okay. Fine. Let's do this properly.

Let's make a real fucking list.

Why Scarletta Mae Desmond has hijacked my brain…

She has matching damage.

Every woman I've ever been with fell into one of two categories. The ones who got scared when they saw what I actually wanted, or the ones who tried to fix me like I was some kind of charity project.

My one real ex girlfriend saw my monster and looked at me like I was diseased. Like I needed therapy, and Jesus, and probably a lobotomy.

The submissives at the clubs played their roles. But underneath, I could see the judgment. The calculation. *How much extra am I getting paid for this freaky shit?*

Scarletta wrote Call of the fucking Labyrinth.

She didn't just tolerate darkness—she cultivated it. Nurtured it. Spent months inside Lyra's head while she got hunted and violated by actual monsters with fur-covered cocks.

That's not someone performing kink. That's someone who lives in the same shadows I do.

I stare at the blank space under my pathetic list.

She craves what I need to give.

My fingers hover over the keys.

This isn't... fuck. This isn't her tolerating my shit. Isn't her playing along because that's what good subs do. Isn't performance art for my benefit.

She *needs* it.

Forty-seven goddamn stories. Every single protagonist the same—begging to be owned, broken down, rebuilt by someone who sees straight through to the ugly parts. She wrote it over, and over, and over again.

The desperation for someone who doesn't love you *despite* the darkness but *because* of it.

That's not research. That's not creative exploration.

That's a manifesto written in a thousand different scenarios, screaming the same truth: *I need this, I need this, I need this.*

She needs dominance the exact same way I need to give it.

Not endured or accommodated.

Necessary.

Which means she doesn't pity me.

That's the big one, isn't it? The one that fucking matters.

Most women who enter my game see what I actually am and look at me like I'm broken. Like I'm damaged goods that need fixing.

Scarletta saw everything and said, *Yes, please. More.*

The cameras in her apartment, the orchestrated scenarios, the elaborate submission frameworks—these are all things she *craves*.

She looked at my darkness and recognized her own reflection.

In fact, she's been writing my exact psychology for years.

Before I existed in her life.

Before she knew my name.

Every protagonist begging to be watched, stalked, owned by someone who sees through the performance. Every villain who builds elaborate scenarios just to prove the heroine wants exactly what terrifies her most.

She documented my architecture without knowing I was real.

I stop typing.

My hand moves to my chest without thinking, pressing against the shirt fabric covering ink I've carried for years.

Her face.

Every goddamn piece. Every woman bound, gagged, displayed—all wearing *her* features. The curve of her jaw. The vulnerable slope of her neck. Those eyes that shift between green and brown depending on the light.

I dreamed her into existence and carved her into my skin before she ever typed the words that would obsess me.

Before she became ScarletSins.

Before DarkDesires.

Before *anything*.

I tattooed a fantasy woman who turned out to be real.

I don't understand this.

I don't believe in fate.

I believe in data. Patterns. Probability distributions. Control over variables.

So either:

A) The universe bent probability into something statistically impossible, orchestrating our collision through mechanisms I can't comprehend or control.

Or:

B) I'm genuinely, clinically insane. My obsession with her writing triggered some psychotic break where I retroactively convinced myself the ink matches her features when it doesn't. Classic confirmation bias dressed up as destiny.

Both explanations terrify me equally.

I can't choose between them.

Don't want to.

Because if it's A, I have no control.

And if it's B, I never did.

I have no one.

Associates, employees., members of The Scales, yes.

But no one who *knows* me.

Scarletta does.

She's seen the worst parts of me and yes, the Maze broke us. But… it also connected us.

Which means something.

I'm not less alone, but the isolation feels less absolute.

Because she exists.

Because someone finally saw me completely.

Even if she can't stay, *she exists*.

The cursor blinks on the screen, waiting for me to finish the list.

But there's nothing left to say.

The list is bullshit.

All of it—the surveillance schedules, the operational assessments, the careful documentation of her flaws and my justifications. I'm not building a case. I'm not making a rational decision.

I'm trying to logic my way into something that exists beyond reason.

You can't spreadsheet your way into love. Can't risk-assess it. Can't control the variables until the outcome becomes predictable.

Love is the thing that makes you willing to burn everything down.

I lean back in the seat, letting the words form inside my head where they're real but still contained.

I love her.

Not obsession. Not possession.

Actual, genuine, terrifying love.

The kind that unmakes you completely.

The kind I have no idea how to survive.

CHAPTER 9
SCARLETTA

This is day ten.

Ten days. That's how long I've been meeting Ryan at the gym for personal training. His goal to make me so fuckable, every man within two hundred miles will be lining up to ask me out, wasn't a euphemism.

He literally meant it.

And he's been punishing my body ever since.

With my absolute permission.

It's not a spanking, there are no nipple clamps or cuffs. He's been… I would not say distant. But he has been professional.

He'll let certain things slip—like that fuckable comment. Or the other day, when I was doing weighted squats and focusing on my form in the floor-length mirror that runs the entire length of the free weights section, he positioned himself behind me, arms crossed, watching my reflection with an intensity that made my thighs tremble for reasons that had nothing to do with the barbell across my shoulders.

When I finished my set and straightened, catching his eyes in the glass, he said, "Your ass looks really good when you squat. I've been watching it in the mirror. I'm gonna put one up in front of you next time, at just the right angle so you can see what I do." Just like that. Matter-of-fact. Professional tone. But his gaze lingered half a second too long before he turned away to adjust the weight rack.

Which seems normal, if you are normal.

But if you're a person who lives and breathes the D/s lifestyle—who understands it down to your bones—the mirror becomes something else entirely.

It transforms from a simple reflective surface into an erotic tool, a psychological weapon, a method of control. It's about being forced to witness your own submission, to see yourself through your Dominant's eyes, to watch your body respond in ways you can't hide or deny.

And my mind immediately went to the gyno table in Caleb's playroom.

How he positioned me on that cold leather surface, securing each limb before spreading my legs wide in those metal stirrups.

He made me watch in the mirror as he penetrated my pussy with that cheap blue Bic pen.

The same pen from my story. The same deliberate, clinical movements. The same psychological warfare disguised as medical examination, exactly the way I'd written it in The Appointment, down to the smallest detail.

The humiliation of it, the wrongness of it, the fact that something so mundane could be transformed into an instrument of such exquisite degradation—all of it played out in perfect detail in that mirror.

I force Caleb out of my mind.

I'm completely over Caleb. Ryan is the one commanding my attention now, filling the spaces in my head that used to belong to someone else. The other day he complimented my new sports bra. He said he liked the colors, coral and black, that they really gave me a 'good outline'.

I've replayed those words approximately fifty times since he said them.

It's maybe not entirely uncommon to comment on a woman's upper body athletic wear at the gym. People talk about brands, about moisture-wicking fabric, about whether Lululemon is worth the insane price tag.

But Ryan's comment wasn't about the brand or the fabric technology.

It was about what the sports bra did for my body, which means it was about my body itself. Which means—and I'm not imagining this—he was looking at my breasts.

Studying them, even.

Okay, fine. Maybe it's just me and my perpetually dirty mind interpreting Ryan's words to be something more than just casual gym pep talk. But he's the one who started it.

He chose those specific words. 'Good outline.' Not 'cute bra' or 'nice color choice' or any of the thousand neutral things he could have said that wouldn't have made my brain spiral exactly where it's spiraling now.

Good outline.

Does this phrase not inherently imply a specific, deliberate shape?

One that includes not just the breasts themselves but how they're positioned, how they're presented, how they're held?

And isn't posture—the way a woman carries herself, the angle of her shoulders, the lift of her chin, the arch of her spine—something a Dominant would naturally notice?

Because I think it is.

I think most men see a woman's chest and think, 'Nice tits,' and that's the complete beginning and end of their cognitive process. They don't analyze why they like them, don't break down the specific elements that create the attraction.

Or maybe—if they're slightly more articulate than the average gym bro—they can identify that the upturned point of the nipple is what draws their eye. Something I definitely have, especially in this particular sports bra with its thin, unpadded cups that hide absolutely nothing.

But they're not thinking about posture. About the way good posture creates the foundation for everything else—the lift, the shape, the outline that Ryan specifically commented on.

Which is the *real* reason aesthetically pleasing breasts exist in the first place, regardless of size or shape.

And Ryan noticed.

I think he's playing it professionally distant.

Not exactly waiting for me to make the first move, he's dropping hints. But he *is* the gym owner and I am a client. Like a real client now, because I bought three months of personal training.

And yeah, one could be cynical and say he's complimenting me because he wanted me to buy the three-month training package.

But I'm his only client at the moment.

He doesn't do that any more. He has a whole crew of trainers to manage the personal training.

So what else should I think?

He obviously likes me.

We banter and laugh as he trains me.

And he touches me. Not anything inappropriate—never anything that crosses a professional line—but he's not shy about making contact when he's correcting my form during a lift.

Sometimes the touches linger just a fraction longer than strictly necessary. Sometimes his hand settles on my lower back with a firmness that feels deliberate, intentional. Sometimes his fingers wrap around my wrist to adjust my grip on the barbell, and his thumb brushes against my pulse point in a way that makes me hyperaware of the contact.

It's always appropriate. Always explainable. Always just

on the edge of professional distance without ever quite stepping over.

But god, do I *wish* he'd step over that line.

I'm dying—actively, desperately dying—for this man to touch me inappropriately. To let one of those lingering hand placements drift lower. To let his fingers tighten on my hip instead of my shoulder. To look at me like he wants to do something other than correct my deadlift form.

Almost seven months now.

Seven months with no sex.

I've started masturbating again, so that's progress, I guess. That's something. That's movement in a forward direction.

But it's not the same.

Not the same, Scarletta?

Before Caleb, you went years without sex and barely noticed. You were fine with self-touch. You functioned. What's different now?

Right. Yeah. I get that. I understand the logical inconsistency here.

But you can't just go from zero to eleven and then back to zero again, can you?

You can't experience something that intense, that all-consuming, that physically and psychologically transformative, and then just... pretend it never happened.

Pretend your body doesn't remember.

Pretend you don't have a new reference point for what touch can feel like, what desire can do to you.

It's set a whole new baseline. A whole new standard. A whole new bar that regular human interaction can't seem to clear.

And that's the problem, isn't it?

I like... weird sex. And Ryan might be the first man I've encountered since... the maze, that could give me more of what I'm after.

He's built like someone who could pin me down. Who

could hold me in place if I tried to squirm away. Who knows what his body can do and isn't afraid to use it.

And he's giving me signals that he's interested. That he's noticed me. That those lingering touches and the deliberate eye contact aren't accidental.

So maybe I should do something about it.

Maybe I should approach him. Stop waiting. Stop hoping he'll escalate. Take some kind of action instead of just... showing up and hoping proximity does the work.

But what the hell would I even say?

How do you signal to someone that you're into the kind of sex that requires negotiation? That you don't just want missionary with the lights off? That you need something darker, something harder, something that involves words like *consensual* and *safeword* in the same conversation?

Do I just walk up to him after my next session and say, "Hey, Ryan, you got any workouts that might help with, say, lowering my gag reflex? Asking for a friend. The friend is me."

Or maybe, "Is there some special routine I could do that might prepare my ass for penetration? Like flexibility training? Core strength? I feel like there's got to be a muscle group involved here that I'm neglecting."

Yeah. Great plan. Really subtle.

And it doesn't help that he looks like he's got a perpetual chub going on beneath those joggers he wears.

Like, it's *always* there. Every single time I see him. Morning, afternoon, doesn't matter—there's a visible outline pressing against the fabric, a ridge that catches the light sometimes when he shifts his weight or leans back against the counter.

I mean, maybe it's not a chub. Maybe it's just—maybe his cock is genuinely that size when it's soft. Maybe that's just what he's working with baseline. Which would mean when he's actually hard, when he's actually aroused, it's probably—

Massive.

Like, genuinely intimidating. Like, I-don't-know-if-that-would-even-fit massive. Like, that-could-be-a-problem-and-I-don't-know-if-I'd-care massive.

And now that I've noticed it, I can't *stop* noticing it.

Every time I walk past the front desk, every time he comes over to adjust a machine setting or ask if I need help with my form, my eyes flick down for half a second before I can stop myself. I don't mean to. It's compulsive at this point. Intrusive thought made visual.

And the worst part is… I think he knows I've noticed.

Because sometimes when I glance up after one of those half-second slips, he's watching me. Not smiling, not smirking—just watching. Waiting to see if I'll look again.

It's hard to tune out.

Impossible, actually.

"Hey, Scarletta?"

I turn, blushing. Because it's Ryan. He's striding towards me with purpose. His cock bouncing beneath his gray sweats.

Do not look. *Do not look.*

It takes every ounce of restraint I have to focus on his face. "Hey, hi. What's up?" *Look at his eyes, Scarletta. His eyes.*

"I've got a question for you."

"Oh," I say. *Please, let this question be, Would you like me to clamp your nipples for today's workout?*

"How would you like to train with me for a special project?" Ryan says. "It's something I'm developing. New program. Still in the testing phase."

I blink at him. My brain's trying to process words but it's stuck somewhere around *train with me* and *special* and honestly, I'm still thinking about his dick.

He mistakes my silence for hesitation. "I need someone who can handle intensity. Someone who won't quit halfway through." His eyes hold mine. "I think that's you."

I still don't say anything. Just stare at him like my vocabulary's been deleted.

"Come on," he says, jerking his head toward the back of the gym. "I'll show you what I mean."

I follow him. Obviously I follow him. What else am I going to do? Say no to a special project with the perpetual chub man?

He walks past the weight racks, past the cardio equipment, down a hallway I've never noticed before. There's a door at the end. Double doors, actually. Industrial looking. He pulls a key from his pocket and unlocks them.

The doors swing open.

Holy shit.

The space is massive. High ceilings with exposed beams. Concrete floor. All the walls are covered with acoustic tiles. The room's mostly empty except for equipment positioned in the center.

And when I say equipment, I mean—

There's a TRX rig mounted to one of the ceiling beams. Professional grade. Multiple straps hanging down. Numerous attachment points.

A modified massage table sits off to the side—except it's not a massage table. Not really. Not with those stirrups fixed at one end, positioned at a precise angle that makes my stomach flip. Anchor points run along the sides at regular intervals, small steel loops welded to the frame. Not decorative. Functional. The kind of thing that doesn't exist in a normal gym setup.

A huge mirror propped against the far wall. Not mounted yet. Angled directly toward the equipment.

Five tripods scattered around the space, positioned at different angles like whoever uses them has been refining their setup for months. Each one has a camera mount. Phone mounts too. A ring light sitting on the floor near the table, the professional kind streamers use, not some cheap Amazon circle.

Everything's organized. Intentional. Not random workout equipment someone's playing with—this is a *production setup*.

A clipboard sits on a folding chair near the table. Against the far wall, a tall storage cabinet stands closed—industrial gray metal with a padlock looped through the handle but hanging open.

I stand there in the middle of the space, trying to process what I'm seeing.

The empty floor stretches around me, too much deliberate nothing.

Every single piece of equipment has been positioned with a goal in mind.

The angles between the tripods and the table aren't random.

The mirror placement isn't accidental.

The ring light's distance from the stirrups is measured.

Even the way the TRX straps hang down creates a specific visual frame.

This isn't someone fucking around with home gym equipment.

This is a film studio.

A production setup designed for one very specific purpose.

I turn to Ryan.

"What is this?"

CHAPTER 10
CALEB

Birds have been spies longer than any intelligence agency existed.

Ancient Romans examined their flight patterns before battle—augury, they called it. Reading the will of the gods through avian movement. Except it wasn't divine intervention. It was reconnaissance. Birds fly high, see everything, report back to gods who could understand.

The Norse had Huginn and Muninn—Odin's ravens. Thought and Memory. Flew across the world each day, returned to whisper secrets in their master's ear. Every culture has a version. Messenger birds. Oracle birds. Birds that watch and tell.

They didn't need cameras or satellites.

They already had wings.

Ryan Adamson.

Thirty-four years old.

Six-two, 190 pounds.

Dark brown hair, short on the sides, a little longer on top.

Brown eyes.

Square jaw, straight nose, slight cleft in his chin.

Good genetics.

Covered in bird tattoos that tell a story about love—intricate and highly custom.

So it is, ironically, the birds that give him away. Because the art on his body has a very particular style.

Just like the work on mine.

But I didn't use the same inkologist for every piece. My theme is… specific. I didn't want any single tattoo artist sitting with me long enough to start studying the theme. Didn't want them wondering what kind of man inks his body up with images of sexual domination.

One artist, one piece, then find another. That's how I did it. So the canvas of my torso, arms, thighs—every available surface—represents a carefully curated gallery. The styles vary deliberately, wildly even.

I wasn't interested in coherence. I rather like the chaos. It's an interesting side to my personality, I think. It reveals a spontaneity in me that almost never surfaces elsewhere.

Ryan Adamson didn't have the same one-and-done mentality when he commissioned his ink. He was committed to his inkologist in more ways than one.

Her name was Posie Little.

I last saw Posie Little three years ago. She was inking up Scarletta's face on my body. It's a throat fuck scene. One of my favorites, actually, that sits right below my sternum. I see it in the mirror every day.

Posie nailed the look of erotic exaltation in the eyes. The stretch and bulge of the throat. My hands on both sides of Scarletta's face.

Sometimes, just looking at that piece gets me hard.

Sometimes, I come on the mirror image of it.

Anyway. The point is, I know Posie.

Knew her.

Since she's dead now.

She was local to Jackson Hole—worked in a shop on Cache Street that catered to wealthy clients who wanted art, not flash. Her work was distinctive, recognizable even from across a room.

She had this particular shading technique, a way of layering grey wash that created depth and dimension most artists couldn't replicate.

It gave her pieces an almost three-dimensional quality, like the images were trying to crawl off the skin. Collectors knew her style instantly. Other artists tried to copy it, and failed.

When you saw one of Posie's pieces, you *knew* it was hers.

And everything about the art on Ryan's body says *Posie was here*.

Since she's dead, I couldn't just go in and ask her about the work. But the shop on Cache Street wasn't hers. And it's still open. Stella Six Feathers owns that shop. Local. 24 now. Grew up on the Wind River Indian Reservation. Bought the parlor on Cache Street when she was nineteen after doing four consecutive consensual-non-consents in one year for the auction house.

Stella was one of the first girls to come through and I wanted to make sure she was OK after she 'retired', so I went into the shop two years later to check up on her.

Anonymously, obviously. She didn't know who I was. Didn't know I ran the auction house.

But I like to make sure the girls are getting on well, especially after CNC's, and was delighted to find that Stella had turned her year of rape fantasies into a very lucrative business. She had five other artists working for her.

Posie Little was one of them.

While I was there, I fell in love with Posie's work and booked my first appointment.

This morning, I went back into that shop and started asking questions. Stella, who didn't know me from Adam, but recognized Posie's work when I privately showed her the tattoo Posie did, got immediately chatty about the 'psychopath with the bird tattoos.'

She told me... *a lot.*

And now... I'm starting to think Ryan Adamson might need his scales balanced.

CHAPTER 11
SCARLETTA

"What is this?"

Ryan's grin shifts into something easier. Genuine, almost. "The future." He gestures toward the TRX rig. "This is my prototype. A full-body suspension training program. But not the basic crap you see in other gyms. This is advanced shit, ya know? A personal training program developed by me."

I stare at the modified table with stirrups. The restraint points. The cameras positioned at angles that would capture everything.

He really thinks I'm going to buy that?

Training?

To be fair, Scarletta, you bought the idea of being sold at a sex auction.

Then signed up for a hunt in a maze.

Touché.

"See, I've got this vision," Ryan continues, walking toward the rig with the confidence of someone who's practiced this pitch enough times it sounds genuine. "I'm gonna convert this whole space into a suspension studio. Group classes. Advanced programs. Something no one else in Idaho Falls is offering."

He turns back to me, and his smile is the kind of easy that probably works on most women. Warm. Excited. Like he's letting me in on a secret.

"I've got a big-deal investor meeting tomorrow at noon. Massive money ask. The kind that could make this happen. But they want proof of concept before they commit to the buildout. They need to see it in action."

Of course, they do.

"That's where you come in, button." He winks at me. Actually winks at me. "I need a model. And… like I said when I took you on for training, you're my only client at the moment."

Like he took me on?

He's making it sound like it was my idea. It wasn't. He's the one who came on to me.

Of course, he did, Scarletta. He was setting you up for this.

Obviously, inner monologue. I'm not a complete fucking idiot. I do actually have real-world experience in the realms of performance sex.

I'm not sure what the look on my face is saying right now, but I'm fairly certain it's not what he expected. Because he launches into pitch number two. "I'll pay you." This comes out softer. Lower. "It's not a lot, but… like… ten grand?"

Ten grand.

He's right. To me, ten grand is half of the base pay for the sex auction. And while that *was* filmed, it was filmed by Caleb. Maybe I don't know him that well, but he doesn't come off as the type of man who likes to sell his videos.

And Ryan… *does*.

He makes porn. I'm a hundred-percent certain of it.

"Twenty," Ryan says. "Twenty grand."

"Twenty grand to… act in your presentation?"

"You don't understand the kind of money at stake here, button. It's three million dollars."

"Three million." I look around. "To turn this into a TRX studio?"

"The insurance is insane," he counters.

OK. I can see that he's going to keep this performance going, no matter what. So I decide to cut to the chase. "What do you really want from me, Ryan? Because while I'm definitely interested in what's going on here..." I motion to the equipment, holding eye contact as I do it. "Especially the stirrups on that table."

His mouth falls open.

"I'm not interested in being circulated on some porn site for the general public."

He laughs. It's small, but genuine. "You little fucking fiend. You've done this before."

I shrug. Feeling pretty bold. "Not this specifically, but... yeah. I get paid sometimes. And let me tell you, ten grand is an insult. Also—" I put up a hand before he can counter again, "I don't need the money."

Again, he's stunned. "You... you don't need the money. What are you saying, Scarletta? You'll do this for free?"

"Depends on what 'this' is."

Ryan steps closer, taking my face in his hands, tilting my head up and forcing me to look him in the eye. "I like to dominate. Do you like to submit?"

I'm dying to submit. But I don't say that, obviously. We're negotiating limits. "Only to professionals."

He laughs again. Absolutely delighted. "Well, I've heard that before. How can I be sure that you understand what will happen?" He moves one hand down my jaw, and begins playing with my lip. "How do I know you won't chicken out?"

He pushes a finger inside my mouth. Placing it firmly on my tongue.

I let him.

Then I answer with his finger in my mouth. It comes out

warbled and weird. "I'll show you." But that's the point. This is a humiliation play. Making me talk around his probing finger is meant to degrade me.

It's clever, I'll give him that.

And hot. I like it.

He pushes his finger deeper towards the back of my throat —not quite enough to gag me but enough to press against that sensitive spot that makes my eyes water—and something inside me just... snaps.

It's not gradual. It's not gentle. It's a sudden, violent rupture of control.

Maybe it's the seven months without sex. Maybe it's the months before that of white-knuckled masturbation sessions I haven't allowed myself since leaving the island. Maybe it's the accumulated weight of every suppressed impulse, every stifled fantasy, every orgasm I've denied myself because letting go meant remembering what it felt like when Caleb made me come apart.

Whatever it is, the arousal doesn't build—it detonates.

One second I'm standing there with his finger lodged in my mouth, trying to maintain some semblance of composure, of negotiation, of control over this situation.

The next second, a jolt of pure, concentrated pleasure slams through my body with such violent intensity that my knees buckle.

My eyes slam shut—not a slow flutter but a hard, involuntary clench as the sensation crashes over me in waves too powerful to process. A moan tears out of my throat, muffled and obscene around his finger, and my head tips back without my permission, exposing the vulnerable line of my throat as the orgasm rips through me like lightning striking dry kindling.

It's over in seconds—sharp, brutal, utterly devastating.

And then the realization hits me with almost the same force as the climax itself.

I just... came.

From a finger in my mouth. From being degraded. From *this*.

The shock of it leaves me frozen, trembling, barely breathing as the aftershocks pulse through my core and my brain scrambles to catch up with what my body just did without asking permission.

"What the fuck just happened?" Ryan's voice comes out hoarse, ragged—each word scraping through the same breathless hitch that's shredding my own composure. "What the fuck did you just do?"

The question hangs between us like a lit fuse, crackling with the same electric charge that's still coursing through my veins, and I can see it written all over his face—the shock, the hunger, the dawning realization that whatever boundary we just crossed, there's no going back now.

I close my eyes and hold still for a breathless second—pulse hammering, cheeks flushed—forcing myself to gather the scattered pieces of what just happened. My mind swims in the after effects of the orgasm as I try to anchor myself back into the moment instead of dissolving entirely.

Then, slowly—deliberately—I pry my eyes open and lock onto his gaze.

His finger is still lodged against my tongue, thick and intrusive, forcing my jaw wide. I don't pull away. I lean into it. Let him feel the vibration of my voice around the digit pinning my mouth open.

"I jus' came," I whisper—garbled, slurred, utterly shameless.

"You little fiend." He looks at me for a moment, moving his finger inside my mouth. Then hurriedly says, "May I check you?"

The question hits me like a second climax I wasn't prepared for, and my entire body clenches reflexively—knees threatening to buckle, core spasming around nothing, breath stuttering out in a broken gasp.

The sheer audacity of him *asking* sends another vicious pulse of arousal through me before I can even attempt to wrestle it down.

Oh god.

I'm going to come again. Right here. Just from *words*.

That's how desperately starved I am. I fight to keep myself upright, coherent, *functional*.

His finger is still pressed flat against my tongue, pinning my mouth open like he owns it—owns *me*—and maybe that's what finally tips me over the edge. The sheer weight of that control. The casual, unflinching dominance radiating off him in waves.

I force myself to breathe. To focus. To answer him.

"Yes," I manage—barely more than a whisper, slurred and messy and trembling with the effort of holding myself together. "Yes. Please."

Immediately, his hand abandons my mouth and plunges into my leggings—no warning, no hesitation, no gentle exploration. Just a direct, ruthless invasion that makes me jolt like I've been electrified.

His fingers slide between my folds with obscene ease, finding me soaked through, drenched to the point of absurdity, and the wet sound of his touch moving through all that arousal is *mortifying*. My entire body flushes hot with shame even as another vicious pulse of want rolls through me.

Then he laughs.

Not a chuckle. Not a dark huff of amusement.

A real laugh—deep, genuine, *delighted*—and it reverberates through the narrow space between us like thunder.

"You fucking whore," he says, voice rich with astonishment and something darker, something hungry. "You actually *came*. Jesus Christ, Scarletta. You're so fucking wet I could—"

He cuts himself off, apparently too fascinated by his discovery to finish the thought. His fingers swirl lazily through the mess between my legs, exploring the evidence of my humiliation with the clinical thoroughness of someone cataloging a particularly interesting specimen.

Circling my entrance. Dragging upward to flick lightly over my oversensitive clit—making me gasp and flinch—then sliding back down through the slick heat again.

He's *playing* in it.

Savoring it.

Making sure I feel every second of his examination.

Then, just as abruptly as he invaded, he withdraws—pulling his hand free with another obscene wet sound that makes my face burn even hotter.

I'm moaning, unable to hide my disappointment.

He brings his glistening fingers up to my face—holding them deliberately in my line of sight so I can see the evidence of what my body did, what it betrayed—and watches my expression with dark, unhurried fascination as he traces them across my skin.

Starting at my left temple.

Dragging down over my eyelid with excruciating slowness, forcing it closed beneath the warm, humiliating wetness.

Then smearing my own slick arousal down my cheek in a slow, deliberate stripe that feels like a brand.

Marking me.

Claiming ownership of my shame.

Making absolutely certain I understand exactly what I am —what I've become—under his touch.

The scent hits me immediately. Musky, and undeniable, and *mine*. My stomach twists with mortification even as another traitorous pulse of heat flares low in my belly, responding to the degradation like it's exactly what I've been craving all along.

I can't look away from him.

Can't close my other eye.

Can't do anything but stare up at his face while he paints me with proof of my own desperation, his expression so darkly satisfied I almost come again.

"Can I fuck you, Scarletta?" he breathes. "Right now. No pretenses. No performance. No proof of concept bullshit."

I swallow hard. Then… before the yes is even out of my mouth, he's got me by the hair. Fisting it. Holding me locked in his grip.

I gasp, a jolt of fear… then… *arousal*. Pure arousal. "Yes," I say. "Fuck me."

The words barely clear my lips before he's moving—yanking me forward by my hair with enough force to make my scalp sting, guiding me toward the modified table with the stirrups like I'm a thing that needs directing instead of a person who can walk.

I stumble. Catch myself. Let him maneuver me exactly where he wants me.

My body is screaming *yes* louder than any rational thought trying to surface. Seven months. Seven months without this—without someone taking control, without the weight of surrender settling over me like a drug I've been white-knuckling my way through withdrawal from.

Ryan spins me around so my back is to the table, still holding my hair in that brutal grip that makes my pussy clench reflexively. His other hand goes to my waist, fingers digging in hard enough to bruise as he lifts me—not gently, not carefully—and drops me onto the padded surface.

The stirrups loom on either side of me like a promise.

"Legs up," he commands, his voice rough and authoritative in a way that bypasses every defense mechanism I've carefully constructed over the past seven months.

I obey without thinking. Automatic. Muscle memory from a different life, a different version of myself who knew exactly what she craved and stopped apologizing for it.

My feet slide into the stirrups, and Ryan immediately adjusts them—pulling, spreading, locking my ankles into position so my legs are splayed wide and completely exposed. Vulnerable in a way that should terrify me but instead sends another vicious pulse of arousal straight to my core.

He steps back. Studies me.

And I realize with a sudden, disorienting clarity that I'm still fully clothed. Sports bra. Leggings. Sneakers now trapped in professional-grade stirrups.

This isn't the slow, sensual undressing I've written about a thousand times. This is something rawer. More desperate.

This is exactly what you need.

Ryan's fingers hook into the waistband of my leggings—not gently testing, not asking permission—and he *rips*. Not pulls them down, not slides them off with careful consideration. He tears them. Right down the center seam between my legs, the sound of splitting lycra obscenely loud in the quiet room.

The material gives way with surprising ease, splitting from waistband to crotch in one violent motion that sends a shock of adrenaline straight through my system.

Cool air hits my exposed skin as the ruined fabric falls away on either side, leaving me bare and exposed, except for the thin strip of my underwear—which is so soaked through it's practically transparent anyway.

He doesn't bother with those either. Just hooks two fingers under the elastic at my hip and *tears*, the delicate lace giving way like tissue paper. Then the other side. The ruined underwear joins my destroyed leggings, nothing but scraps of fabric pooling uselessly around my hips.

I should protest. Should say something about how those leggings cost seventy dollars and I just bought them last week. Should care that he's destroying my clothes with the same casual brutality he used on my carefully constructed walls.

But I don't.

I can't.

Oh god.

My pussy is completely visible now—swollen, glistening, still dripping from the orgasm I had standing up barely two minutes ago. The humiliation of being on display like this should make me want to close my legs, cover myself, *hide.*

Instead, I'm so wet I can feel it leaking down between my cheeks, pooling on the table beneath me.

Ryan notices. Of course he notices.

"Jesus Christ, Scarletta." His voice comes out strangled, reverent, like he's discovered something holy and profane at the same time. "Look at you."

I can't look. I refuse to look. If I turn my head toward the massive mirror positioned deliberately to capture every angle, I'll see exactly what he sees—my body spread obscenely wide, my pussy exposed and desperate, my face flushed with shame and arousal I can't separate anymore.

Don't look. Don't you fucking dare look.

But I do.

I turn my head.

And there I am—platinum blonde hair tangled from his grip, sports bra still covering my breasts, legs locked wide in stirrups, hidden behind tattered leggings. But what's between them, open, bare, and dripping.

I look like a pornographic medical diagram. Like one of my own characters. Like every shameful fantasy I've ever written and immediately deleted before anyone could see.

This is who you are.

The thought hits me with the same brutal clarity as the orgasm did.

Not the woman who pretends to be normal. Not the writer who hides behind anonymous usernames. Not the girl who ghosts men before the third date because letting them get close means they might discover what she really wants.

This.

This is who I am.

Ryan's hands go to his waistband, shoving his joggers down just enough to free his cock—thick and hard and exactly as intimidating as I suspected when I was obsessing over the constant bulge he walked around with.

He doesn't bother undressing completely. Doesn't waste time with foreplay, or preparation, or asking if I'm ready.

He just positions himself between my spread legs, one hand wrapped around his cock, pumping slowly while his eyes stay locked on my exposed pussy with a hunger so raw it makes my breath catch.

He's *massive.*

Thick, and long, and not even fully hard yet—still swelling in his fist as he stares at me like I'm the first meal he's seen after weeks of starvation.

The head is flushed dark, precum already beading at the tip, and watching him stroke himself while studying every glistening fold between my legs, sends another vicious pulse of arousal straight through my core.

Oh god. Oh fuck.

I should be scared. Should be calculating whether something that size will even fit inside me after seven months of nothing. Should be doing the responsible thing and asking about condoms or at least slowing this down enough to think.

But I don't.

I can't.

Because I'm dying for this—dying to feel something real, and brutal, and overwhelming enough to drown out every careful, controlled moment I've endured since leaving Story Island.

Ryan's other hand comes down to my hip, gripping hard enough that I know there'll be finger-shaped bruises tomorrow. He angles himself, positioning the thick head of his cock at my entrance—not gently testing, not easing in slowly—just lining himself up like he's preparing to claim what he's already decided belongs to him.

Then he *jams* into me.

No warning. No gradual stretch. Just one brutal thrust that splits me open around his thickness and makes me cry out—a sharp, broken sound that echoes off the walls of this hidden room.

Pain.

It hits me first—searing, and immediate, and so intense my entire body locks up around the intrusion. He's too big. Too thick. My body hasn't been used like this in months and it's fighting the invasion even as my pussy floods with more wetness, trying desperately to accommodate him.

But underneath the pain—woven through it like a thread of gold in dark fabric—is something else.

Delicious.

The word surfaces in my mind unbidden, shocking in its accuracy.

This hurts. This is exactly what I need. This is everything I've been craving without knowing how to ask for it.

Ryan doesn't stop. Doesn't give me time to adjust or breathe or process what's happening. He pulls back slightly— just enough that I feel the drag of his cock against my sensitive inner walls—then slams back in deeper, forcing another few inches inside me with a grunt of satisfaction that sounds almost feral.

"Fuck," he breathes, voice gone ragged. "You're so fucking tight."

I can't respond. Can't form words around the sensation consuming me.

My hands fly up instinctively, grabbing at the edges of the table, fingers scrabbling for purchase against the padded surface as he fucks into me again. And again. Each thrust brutal and claiming and exactly what my body has been screaming for.

The pain starts to shift. Morphing into something deeper, more complex—still there but now threaded through with pleasure so intense it makes my vision blur at the edges.

This. This is what I've been missing.

Not gentle lovemaking. Not careful exploration with someone who treats me like I might break. But this—raw, and desperate, and so physically overwhelming that there's no room left in my brain for the constant spiral of self-judgment and shame.

There's only sensation.

His cock stretching me impossibly wide. The obscene wet sounds of him fucking into my drenched pussy. The way my legs tremble uselessly in the stirrups as he uses me exactly how he wants.

I force my eyes open—didn't even realize I'd squeezed them shut—and look down the length of my body.

The sight nearly breaks me.

My sports bra still covering my breasts. My legs spread wide and locked in place. Ryan between my thighs. And his cock—thick and glistening with my arousal—disappearing into my body with each brutal thrust.

You're getting exactly what you wrote about. Every shameful fantasy. Every dark craving you were too afraid to admit.

The thought sends another vicious pulse through my core, my pussy clenching reflexively around his thickness in a way that makes him groan.

"That's it," he growls, fingers digging harder into my hip. "Squeeze my cock. Show me how much you fucking need this."

I do need this.

I need to be split open, and claimed, and fucked so hard I can't think about anything except the overwhelming physical reality of being *used*.

Ryan shifts his angle slightly—pulling back farther this time before slamming in with enough force to make the entire table shudder beneath me—and something inside me gives way.

Not breaking. Not tearing.

Just... surrendering.

My body stops fighting the invasion and starts accepting it, accommodating the brutal stretch, welcoming the pain-laced pleasure that's building with each thrust.

And suddenly he's deeper. Impossibly deeper. Buried inside me so completely I can feel him everywhere—pressing against places that make stars explode behind my eyelids, filling me so thoroughly there's no space left for anything except *this*.

"Fuck yes," he breathes, satisfaction dripping from every syllable. "There you go. Take it all."

I'm moaning—desperate, broken sounds I don't recognize —as he establishes a rhythm. Pulling out until just the thick head remains inside me, then slamming back in with punishing force that makes my entire body jolt against the restraints.

The stirrups keep my legs spread wide no matter how much I tremble. The table holds me perfectly positioned for his use. And I'm helpless to do anything except take what he's giving me.

"Shit," he groans. "Fuck, Scarletta. I'm gonna come, you little fiend. Ten goddamn minutes and I'm at your fucking mercy."

He reaches forward with one hand, fingers spreading wide as they cup the back of my neck. The grip is possessive, demanding, as he hauls me upward off the table—forcing my spine to arch as my entire upper body lifts toward him.

"See?" he demands through gritted teeth. "See what you do to me?"

I do see.

God help me, I see *everything*.

"If I come," he says, his breath coming in harsh, ragged bursts that match the rhythm of his thrusts, "you come too." His hand releases my neck, fingers sliding up into my hair instead. He winds his fist into the strands—not gently, not carefully—just twisting until my scalp burns and I gasp. "Do you hear me?"

He yanks me closer, my face tilting up to meet his as he leans down. Then his mouth crashes against mine—brutal, consuming—all teeth, and tongue, and desperate hunger. He bites my lower lip hard enough to sting.

"Do you *fucking* hear me, little fiend?"

"Yes," I gasp against his mouth. "Yes, I—"

But the word barely escapes before his hand slides between us—rough, demanding—and his thumb finds my clit.

The pressure is immediate. Perfect. Devastating.

He circles once. Twice.

And I *detonate*.

My orgasm hits like a physical blow—ripping through me with such brutal intensity that my entire body locks up around his cock. Every muscle seizing. My pussy clenching so hard around his thickness that he groans into my open mouth.

"Fuck—" Ryan's voice breaks. "Fuck, Scarletta—"

His rhythm shatters. Three more brutal thrusts—desperate and erratic—then he yanks himself out with a guttural sound that's half curse, half prayer as I slam back against the table.

His hand wraps around his cock—slick with my arousal—and he aims at my stomach as he comes.

Hot ropes of come paint my skin. Thick, and white, and obscene across my exposed stomach. Hitting the underside of my sports bra. Spattering across my ribs and chest.

One particularly strong pulse arcs higher—landing on my chin.

Oh god.

I'm marked. Completely. Undeniably.

Still trembling from my orgasm, still locked in the stirrups with my legs spread wide, covered in his release like some kind of depraved art installation.

I just lie there, chest heaving, pussy still clenching around nothing, his come cooling on my skin as my brain slowly comes back online.

Ryan recovers first. His breathing evening out while mine still comes in ragged gasps. He leans forward, one hand bracing against the table beside my head, and kisses me. Not brutal this time. Gentle and tender.

When he pulls back, there's a wicked grin spreading across his face.

"Dirtiest little fucking button ever," he murmurs against my lips.

The nickname is cute. I like it. I like… *him.*

We stay like that for a long moment—him leaning over me, both of us catching our breath, the evidence of what we just did cooling between us.

Then Ryan straightens, adjusting his joggers and pulling them back up over his hips like what just happened was casual. Normal. Something that happens in the back room of his gym every day.

Maybe it does.

Don't think about that.

He walks to a cabinet against the far wall—the kind meant for supplies or equipment—and opens it. Inside, instead of weights or resistance bands, there's merchandise. Iron River Fitness t-shirts and shorts in various sizes, all neatly folded and organized.

He selects a black t-shirt and matching bike shorts, glances at me still spread open on the table, then returns to me with an offering. His satisfaction barely disguised as apology. "Sorry about your clothes," he says, reaching for the stirrup releases.

I'm not.

The restraints pop open and my legs drop—heavy, trembling, completely useless. I don't trust myself to stand yet. Don't trust my body to do anything except continue lying here like a used, thoroughly fucked disaster.

But I sit up so I can change. Ryan watches as I peel off my sports bra—also splattered with his cum—and pull the fresh shirt over my head.

I shimmy into the bike shorts next, my movements clumsy and uncoordinated as sensation slowly returns to my limbs.

When I'm finally decent—or as decent as someone can be after getting fucked raw on an examination table—Ryan leans in again.

This kiss is different. Slower. More deliberate.

Like he's tasting me. Memorizing me.

"Come back tomorrow morning," he murmurs against my lips. "Five AM. We'll go another round." He pulls back from the kiss just enough to meet my eyes. "This time I'll be prepared."

I cannot contain my smile.

He kisses me one more time—quick and claiming—then straightens and walks toward the door.

He doesn't look back. Doesn't wait to see if I need help getting off the table or finding my way out.

Just leaves.

Savor this. Remember every second. You're finally getting what you've been dying for.

So I do…
Because this man is exactly what I need.
No, he's more than that.
Ryan Adamson is exactly what I *want*.

CHAPTER 12
CALEB

Three kills stand out in my memory.

Three kills that remind me exactly what I am.

Three memories that still get me so hard, there's no fucking way I can't jerk off when I think about them.

Case number 5. The twenty-three year old tech billionaire. Venture capital golden boy with a seed-stage portfolio worth nine figures.

Thirty-seven women in six months.

He didn't rape them. Didn't need to. Money bought consent until it didn't, and then his hands were around their throats while he fucked them and they stopped breathing.

I found him in Dubai. Extradited him through channels that don't officially exist.

Chained his hands to his feet—proper hog-tie configuration, stainless steel, no slack. Positioned him so his cock was *right there*. Close enough to taste if he bent far enough.

"Two hours," I told him. "Suck your own dick for two hours, and I'll consider letting you live."

He cried. Begged. Tried to negotiate.

I waited.

He wrapped his lips around his own cock after fifteen minutes of crying like a baby. Desperation makes men flexible in ways anatomy shouldn't allow. I remember the exact way his spine curved. The groans and whimpers from the strain to keep the tip of his dick in his mouth.

I pull out my cock, it's already thick and pulsing. Can't help it. Just the memory makes my hand wrap around my shaft, pre-come already slicking the head when I swipe my thumb over it.

I jerked off that day too. Pumping my fist up and down my shaft while I watched him work. His technique was *terrible*—all teeth and panic—but he managed. For thirty-seven minutes he managed.

Then I walked over and sawed through the base of his cock with a hunting knife.

The blood fountained. Poured down his throat as he choked on his own severed dick.

He drowned in himself.

My hand moves faster now, thumb circling the ridge as I remember the sound he made—wet and gurgling and *final* and shift into the image of the second kill that still makes me hard.

Case number twenty-four. A British woman. Thirty-seven. Opened a boarding school in rural Uganda for "talented young boys."

Talent meant pretty. Meant vulnerable. Meant no one would notice when they disappeared into her private quarters for "special tutoring sessions."

Sixteen confirmed deaths. She killed them after. Afraid of witnesses? Afraid of herself is more likely.

I flew her to Story Island. Told her it was a donor retreat. She believed me because people like her always believe their money makes them untouchable.

The fuck machine was industrial. Pneumatic piston

system, variable speed control, custom twelve-inch attachment I had fabricated specifically for her.

I strapped her down spread eagle. Wrists, ankles, waist, throat. Positioned the machine. Turned it on.

Forty-eight hours.

I'm jerking myself hard now, eyes closed, picturing what I saw when I finally shut it off and slit her throat.

There was... *nothing* left.

Then I picture the crème de la crème of kills.

Case number one. Eighty-three years old. Retired missionary. Respected community elder.

More than a hundred children confirmed. Probably twice that.

Decades of rape and murder hidden behind charitable donations and fucking *prayer vigils*.

My first kill. The one that started everything.

I built the rack myself. Medieval design, modernized with hydraulic tension controls and digital pressure gauges. Precision engineering for maximum suffering.

I strapped him down and explained exactly what was going to happen.

"Your joints will separate first," I told him. "Shoulders, hips, knees. The ligaments tear before the cartilage fails. You'll hear it before you feel it—wet pops, like knuckles cracking but *louder*."

He prayed. Actually fucking prayed while I activated the mechanism.

I was right about the sound.

Shoulders went first. Pop-pop—both at once, symmetrical failure at identical tension points.

His hips took longer. Required more pressure. When they finally gave—

I come.

Hard.

My orgasm rips through me as I remember that sound—the wet *explosion* of his hip joints detonating.

Come spurts over my hand, my stomach, hot and thick as I stroke myself through the aftershocks.

The old man screamed for forty-three minutes before his heart gave out.

I recorded every second.

Still jerk off to it sometimes.

The key code for the door chimes the number sequence. I put my cock away, ignore the sticky come on my hand and shorts, and focus.

Scarletta enters her dark apartment.

She sets her keys and phone on the counter near the door. Doesn't turn on the light. Just stands there for a moment, silhouetted against the window where downtown Idaho Falls glows orange and blue through the glass.

It's almost nine. Late for her. She left around seven. Two hours.

Two hours at a restaurant when she *never* eats at restaurants. Always takes it home. Always retreats to her apartment like the hermit she is.

Was.

Because tonight she stayed. Tonight she sat in public and let strangers see her. Let them watch her eat. Let them approach her table—I'm guessing here, but it's an educated guess based on the new platinum hair and the way men can't stop staring at her now.

She's still wearing the Iron River Fitness t-shirt. Black, fitted, his logo across her tits. The bike shorts—too short, too tight, hugging her ass in a way that makes me angry and turned on at the same time.

I watch her move through her apartment. She doesn't know I'm here. I'm sitting in the chair she never uses, the expensive one that came with the furnished place. Positioned away from the window, deep in shadow where the streetlight can't reach me.

No cameras in this apartment. I gave her that. Privacy. Space. The illusion of freedom.

Didn't mean I couldn't break in.

She walks to the window and looks out at the city. Her shoulders drop. Relaxed. Happy.

She's *happy*.

That realization hits like a fist to the solar plexus.

When she left my limo the day I brought her back from Story Island she wasn't happy. She was shattered. Broken. Traumatized by what I'd shown her.

Seven months. Seven months of watching her try to rebuild herself into someone normal. Someone who could survive without the darkness we both crave.

And now she's happy because some tattooed gym rat wants to fuck her?

Did fuck her?

He did. I don't know for sure, but I know.

And now I need details.

Because Scarletta came out of the gym different than when she went in. Flushed. Walking carefully—the kind of careful that means a woman's been fucked hard enough to feel it hours later.

Wearing his clothes.

Like she's *his*.

Scarletta pulls off the Iron River shirt. Doesn't bother closing the blinds. Just strips it over her head and tosses it on the couch.

No bra underneath. Her tits are perfect. Still perfect. Nipples hardening in the cool air.

I should look away. Should give her this. Privacy. Dignity. The things I claimed I wanted to give her when I said I'd stay away.

I look.

She peels off the bike shorts next. No underwear. I can see the marks on her hips—finger-shaped bruises, already purpling. He grabbed her hard. Held her down.

Marked what's *mine*.

The rage builds slow. Methodical. The way it always does before I kill someone.

Ryan Adamson doesn't know who he's fucking with. Doesn't know the woman he just claimed belongs to me in ways that go deeper than possession. Deeper than ownership.

Scarletta is the only person alive who's seen me completely. Seen the monster behind the mask, and the mask behind the monster, and every ugly fucking layer in between.

And she ran.

She *ran* from me and straight into Ryan's waiting arms because she thinks Ryan is safe. Thinks Ryan is *normal*.

Ryan doesn't torture child traffickers. Doesn't come on corpses or the memory of killing them. Doesn't need darkness the way I need oxygen.

Scarletta walks naked to her bathroom. Closes the door. I hear water running. Shower.

Washing him off. Or maybe not.

Does she likes smelling like his sweat and come?

Every instinct screams at me to walk into that bathroom. To strip. To join her. To fuck her against the tile until she remembers exactly who she belongs to.

But I don't.

I wait.

Because she is mistaken if she thinks this is over.

It's not over.

It will never be over.

Scarletta Mae Desmond is mine.

Just thinking these words—*my good little slut*—is enough to make my cock stiffen again, blood rushing south like my body doesn't give a fuck about dignity or restraint. I don't even hesitate. I reach down, wrap my fingers around my still-sticky shaft, and start stroking again. Slow at first, savoring it. Building.

I never get tired of this. Never get tired of jerking off to her, to the memory of what I've done, to the bodies I've left behind and the way power feels when it's absolute. I could go all day and night if I've got the right fantasy fueling me.

And Scarletta—my beautiful, broken, *mine* Scarletta—is that fantasy.

Everything about her makes me hard these days. Including the way she thinks she can replace me with someone safe, someone *normal*, someone who doesn't see her the way I do.

The way she's in that shower right now, washing Ryan's sweat off her skin, and has no idea I'm sitting here watching her door. Waiting. Hard.

The water stops.

I tense—muscles coiling, breath catching—but I don't stop stroking. My hand keeps moving, slow and deliberate, while I wait. *Waiting*, waiting, *waiting* for her to emerge. My cock throbs in my fist, aching, demanding, and I lean forward slightly, eyes fixed on that bathroom door like it's the only thing in the world that matters.

The door opens.

She steps out wearing nothing but a towel, hair dripping wet, skin flushed pink from the heat. And there's this stupid, blissful smile on her face—the kind of smile that tells me everything I need to know. She's still riding the high of whatever the fuck Ryan gave her.

Still thinking about *him*.

She looks up.

Her eyes land on me.

The smile vanishes.

She *screams*. "What the fuck! Oh, my fucking god, are you serious right now? You broke in—you're *jerking off*? What the actual fuck, Caleb! I told you to leave me the fuck alone!"

I stay absolutely still.

Except for my hand. It pumps harder. Faster. My grip tightens, and I don't look away from her face—not for a second. I want her to see me. I want her to know exactly what she does to me, what she's *always* done to me.

"Well?" She yells, voice cracking with fury and something else—something that sounds like panic. "What the fuck are you doing here?"

"I'm here for you, Scarletta." My voice comes out low, steady, like I'm explaining something simple to a child. "Why else would I be here?"

"You need to leave. Right now!" She points to the door with one shaking hand while the other clutches her towel like it's armor. "Now!"

"You fucked him, didn't you?"

"*What*?" Her face flushes—and I'm not talking about the lingering heat from the shower. I'm talking bright, burning red. Guilt, and indignation, and something else all tangled together.

"You *fucked* him."

"My sex life is none of your business!"

"Did he spread you out on his desk? Did you let him slide his cock into your pussy while you moaned like a good girl?" I keep stroking, grip tightening as I watch her face change. "Did he make you come, baby? Did he pump you full while you told him how good it felt?"

"Stop it."

"I bet he was vanilla as fuck. Missionary position. Maybe he flipped you over if he was feeling *adventurous*." My thumb swipes over the head of my cock, spreading pre-come. "Probably came in three minutes and told you how sexy you are."

Her jaw clenches. "You don't know anything."

"I know you." I lean forward slightly, still working my shaft. "I know what makes your pussy wet. I know what makes you scream. And I *know* Ryan Adamson didn't give you what you actually need."

"Get out of my apartment."

"Not until you tell me."

"Tell you *what*?"

"Did he fuck your throat? Did he make you gag on his cock until tears ran down your face?" My voice drops lower, rougher. "Did he tie you down and edge you until you begged? Or did he just stick his dick in and pump away like every other boring fuck you've had?"

"You want to know?" Scarletta's voice cuts through the space between us. Sharp. Clear. Not trembling anymore.

I stop stroking. My hand freezes mid-shaft, fingers tight around my cock as I look at her. Really look at her.

She's standing straighter now. Chin lifted. The towel clutched in one hand but her posture isn't defensive anymore —it's *defiant*.

"You want to know what Ryan did to me?" She takes a step closer. "Fine. I'll tell you."

My pulse spikes. Every muscle in my body goes rigid.

"He made me come," she says, voice steady, "just by putting his finger in my mouth."

My cock twitches in my grip.

"He told me he wanted to film me. I told him I'd done paid sexual work before. That I wasn't interested in his bullshit pitch. I didn't need money to fuck him. I fuck whoever I want, whenever I want." Another step. She's close enough now I can smell her shampoo—vanilla and something floral. "He asked if I like to submit."

My breathing quickens. I start stroking again. Slow. Controlled.

"I told him I only submit to professionals. And you know what he did?" Her eyes lock onto mine. "He pushed his finger into my mouth. Just shoved it in like I was a whore. And I came. Right there. Fully clothed. Just from his finger."

My hand moves faster.

"He laughed at me. Called me a whore. Asked if he could check my pussy to see if I was telling the truth." She watches my hand pumping my shaft. "I said yes."

"*Fuck,*" I moan...

"He touched me and I came again. On his fingers. Instantly." Her voice drops lower, quieter. Deadly. "He has a table too, Caleb. With stirrups. He locked my ankles in and ripped my clothes off—didn't even bother undressing me properly. Just tore through my leggings like they were tissue paper."

I'm jerking myself hard now, breath coming harsh through my teeth.

"He spread me wide open. Bound. Helpless. Exactly the way I like it." She tilts her head. "And then he fucked me so hard I felt it for hours afterward."

My orgasm builds—pressure coiling tight at the base of my spine, balls drawing up.

"He came all over me. Marked me. Told me to come back tomorrow morning at five AM for round two."

I come.

Hard.

Violently.

My hand works frantically as I spurt across my stomach, my chest, hot ropes of come painting my skin while I stare at her face and hate everything about this moment.

Hate that she's watching. Hate that she told me. Hate Ryan. Hate myself.

Hate that I can't stop.

Love that it's *her* that makes me so sick.

The release doesn't help. Instantly, I'm hard again.

Scarletta notices. Her eyes go wide before she can stop them. Then she looks at me. "You're pathological."

"Absolutely," I moan. Stroking again. Ready to come a third time.

"You're a walking nightmare."

"Yes. A certifiable fucking monster. What's your point."

The incredulous look on her face makes me smile. Then it's my turn.

"You want to know your taste in men, baby?" I keep stroking, slow and deliberate. "Let me tell you. Your taste in men is *me*."

She opens her mouth to protest.

"You begged me to fuck your throat in that cabin. Begged me to make you gag on my cock until you couldn't breathe. You came so hard you blacked out—multiple times—and every time you woke up, you wanted more."

"I don't remember that," she says, but her voice wavers.

"I know you don't. Subspace psychosis, remember? But I recorded everything." My hand moves faster. "You on your knees, choking on my dick, tears streaming down your face while you moaned around my shaft. You bent over the table, spread wide, begging me to fuck your ass. You strapped to the cross, screaming for me to hurt you harder."

"Stop—"

"You came seventeen times in four hours. I counted. You passed out twice from the intensity and woke up *begging* for my cock inside you again." I'm jerking myself hard now, watching her face flush. "You told me you needed it. Needed me to use you like the desperate little slut you are."

"You're disgusting," she spits.

"Says the woman who just fucked her gym trainer with her legs in stirrups."

"At least I can get off without jerking myself like a lonely fucking teenager!"

I grin. Stop stroking just long enough to spread my arms wide—cock standing hard and obscene between my thighs. "I've got more come inside me for you, Scarletta. All you have to do is sit on my lap."

She stops breathing.

Complete stillness. Her chest freezes mid-inhale.

I've won.

"Come here, baby," I say softly, switching tactics. Sweet now. Coaxing. "Let me make you feel good. You know Ryan didn't get you there—not really. Not the way you need."

Her eyes flick to my cock. Back to my face.

"Just walk over here. Drop that towel. Straddle my lap and sink down on my dick." My voice drops lower, intimate. "I'll fill you up so perfectly. Stretch that sweet little pussy the way it's meant to be stretched. You can ride me as slow as you want. Or I'll grab your hips and fuck up into you until you scream."

Her breathing starts again—shallow, rapid.

"I'll rub your clit while you're impaled on me. Make you come so hard you forget Ryan's name. Forget your own name. Just be my good little slut taking exactly what she needs."

Her knuckles go white around the towel.

"All you have to do," I whisper, "is sit. On. My. Lap."

She wants to. Her pussy is probably throbbing so hard, she can't stand it. But she's not going to admit it.

So I'm going to make her admit it.

"You want me, baby," I say softly. "I can see it. Your body knows exactly what it needs."

I stop stroking. Let my hand fall away from my cock, which stands thick and hard between my thighs.

"Come here." My voice drops lower. Gentle now. Coaxing. "Just walk over here. You don't have to do anything you don't want. I promise."

She doesn't move, but she doesn't tell me to fuck off either.

Progress.

"I'll be so careful with you," I continue, keeping my tone soft. Sweet. "I'll kiss your mouth. Touch you gently. Make it good for you." I pause, watching her face. "If that's what you want."

Her nose wrinkles slightly. Just a fraction.

There it is.

"But that's not what you want, is it?" I lean into the chair, spreading my thighs wider. "You don't want gentle. You don't want careful. You want it hard, and rough, and dirty. You want to be used like the good little slut you are."

Her breathing hitches.

I stretch out my hand. Palm up. Beckoning.

"Come here, Scarletta."

She stares at my hand like it's a trap.

It *is* a trap.

"One last time," I say quietly. "Fuck me one last time, and I'll leave. I'll walk out that door and never come back. You can have Ryan, and his vanilla missionary position, and his boring three-minute fucks for the rest of your life."

Her eyes narrow. "You're lying."

"Of course, I'm lying." I keep my hand extended, looking her in the eyes. "I want you. You tick all the boxes, Scarletta. You're my destiny. But I'm not going to force you. Not right now, not ever. But… I'm fixated, you see. Obsessed. And after what you just told me about Ryan, I'll never get over it. If it's true, I'll obsess. Forever. Was it true? What Ryan did? Because if so… don't I deserve a chance?"

"A chance to what?" she snarls.

"To change your mind. To show you how I'm better. How *we* are better."

"Why would I do that? It'll just make you stay."

"No. If you fuck me one last time, I'll leave. I promise. Cross my heart. I'll leave and never come back." I gesture to my lap with my outstretched hand. "You get one last ride on my cock. I get to fill that desperate pussy, knowing I did my best to convince you. And then we're done. Forever. Because if you truly want Ryan, fucking me right now won't change that, right? You'll still want him tomorrow… if… we're not meant to be together."

Scarletta shakes her head. "You're trying to trick me."

"Trick you into what, Scarletta? Either you want to be his, or you don't. Come on, come here. At least let me hold you."

She takes a step forward.

Then another.

I don't move. Don't rush her. Just keep my hand extended, palm up, like I'm offering food to a scared animal.

"You look beautiful," I say softly. Gentle. The way you'd speak to something fragile. "Your hair—the platinum blonde. It suits you perfectly. Makes your eyes look even more incredible."

Her bottom lip trembles.

"You've always been beautiful, Scarletta. Even when you were hiding in that ratty hoodie and living off Lucky Charms. Even when you thought no one saw you." I keep my voice low, soothing. "But this—what you've done over the past six months—it's fucking stunning. You've grown up. Matured. Become the woman you were always meant to be."

A tear slides down her cheek.

"Come here, baby," I whisper. "Let me hold you. Just for a minute. That's all."

She shakes her head, but her feet keep moving forward. One step. Another. Closer.

"You're doing so good," I murmur. Encouraging. Sweet. "Such a good girl. Just a little closer."

Another tear falls. Then another. She's crying now—silent tears streaming down her face while she stands there clutching that towel like it's the only thing keeping her together.

"Sit, Scarletta."

Her knees bend. She lowers herself onto my lap—awkward at first, hesitant, like she doesn't trust this. Doesn't trust me.

But she sits anyway.

I wrap my arms around her immediately. Pull her close against my chest. One hand slides up into that platinum hair

—so soft, so perfect—while the other settles at the small of her back.

"There you go," I breathe against her temple. "Good girl. Such a good little slut."

She breaks.

The sob that tears out of her is raw and desperate and everything I've been waiting for. She buries her face against my shoulder and cries—really cries—while I hold her, and stroke her hair, and tell her how good she is.

"I've got you," I whisper. "Right here. I've got you."

Her whole body shakes with it. Seven months of holding it together, seven months of pretending she's fine, seven months of running—all of it comes pouring out while I sit there and let her fall apart in my arms.

"Shhhh," I soothe, fingers threading through her hair. "You're okay. You're safe."

She's not safe. Not even close. But she needs to hear it anyway.

I rock her slightly. Back and forth. Gentle motion while my hand strokes down her spine, over the curve of her lower back, then up again. Repetitive. Calming. The way you'd comfort a frightened animal.

"So beautiful," I murmur against her hair. "So fucking perfect."

Her crying starts to slow. The sobs become quieter, more controlled. She's getting herself together again—rebuilding those walls brick by brick.

I won't let her.

"One last time," I say softly. "And then I'm gone. I promise."

She pulls back enough to look at me. Her eyes are red, nose running. She's a mess.

She's gorgeous.

"You promise?" Her voice cracks on the words.

"I promise." I stroke her cheek with my thumb, wiping

away tears. "One last time, and then I walk away. I won't come back until you come to me."

She searches my face. Looking for the lie. Looking for the trap.

She won't find it.

Because this time—this one fucking time—I'm telling the truth.

If we're going to be together forever... it has to be her choice.

"This time," I say quietly, holding her gaze, "I will not waver. I'll walk out that door, and I won't come back. Not to your apartment. Not to the gym. Not to the coffee shop." I brush my thumb across her bottom lip. "If you don't come to me, we will never see each other again. I promise."

She wants to believe me. I can see it in her eyes—the desperate, fragile hope that maybe this time I'm actually telling the truth.

I am.

For once in my twisted, fucked-up life, I'm actually telling the truth.

"Okay," she whispers.

I grip her hips—both hands now, firm and claiming—and lift her. She gasps, instinctively wrapping her arms around my neck as I position her directly over my cock.

The towel falls away.

She's naked in my lap. Wet from the shower. Warm, and soft, and everything I've been craving for seven months.

I lower her slowly.

The head of my cock presses against her entrance. She's already wet—so fucking wet—and I slide in easily. Inch by inch. Stretching her. Filling her.

Her head falls back, mouth opening on a silent moan as I sink deeper.

"That's it," I breathe. "Take it, baby. Take every inch."

She does. Her pussy swallows my cock completely until

I'm buried to the hilt, her thighs trembling where they bracket my hips.

I hold her there. Don't move. Just let her feel it—the fullness, the stretch, the way we fit together like we were made for this.

"Fuck," she whimpers.

"One last time," I remind her. My hands tighten on her hips. "Let's make it count."

I stand, gripping her ass with both hands, cock still buried deep. She gasps, wrapping her legs around my waist as I turn and slam her back against the wall.

"*Fuck!*" she cries out.

The impact drives me deeper. Her pussy clenches around my shaft, and I grind against her, pinning her there with my hips.

"You feel that?" I growl against her ear. "Feel how fucking deep I am? How your pussy is stretched around my cock like it was made for me?"

She moans, head falling back. Eyes closed. Mouth open. Completely lost in it.

I pull out almost completely, then slam back in.

"*Yes!*" Her nails dig into my shoulders.

I do it again. Harder. The wet sound of our bodies connecting echoes off the high ceilings.

"This is what you need, isn't it?" I pant, fucking up into her with brutal thrusts. "Not Ryan's mediocre bullshit. Not some vanilla boyfriend who'll treat you like you're normal. You need this. You need me."

"Oh god—"

"Say it." I bite her neck, sucking hard enough to leave a mark. "Tell me what you are."

"Your—*fuck*—your slut—"

"*Good* little slut," I correct, punctuating each word with a thrust. "Mine. All mine. This pussy belongs to me. Always has. Always will."

She's bouncing on my cock now, using the wall for leverage, riding me with desperate need. Her tits bounce with every thrust, nipples hard, and pink, and perfect.

"You think Ryan can fuck you like this?" I grab her throat—not squeezing, just holding. Claiming. "Think he knows how to make you come so hard you black out? Think he understands what you need?"

"No—*no*—"

"Fucking right he doesn't." I slam into her harder, feeling my orgasm building. "Only me. Only I know how to wreck this perfect little pussy. Only I know how filthy you really are."

Her pussy flutters around me. She's close.

"You're going to come on my cock," I command. "Right now. While I fill you up. And every time you see Ryan at that gym, you'll remember who you really belong to."

"*Caleb—*"

"Come, Scarletta. *Now.*"

She detonates. Her entire body goes rigid, pussy clamping down on my shaft like a vice as she screams my name. The orgasm tears through her, violent and absolute.

I fuck her through it, chasing my own release. But this isn't how it ends. if this really is the last time—it isn't, but I could be wrong, stranger things have happened—if it's the last time, then she's going to finger herself relentlessly for the rest of her life to the memory of it.

As soon as her clenching stops—as soon as that vicious grip on my shaft relaxes—I pull out completely. She makes a wounded little sound, confused, still shaking from the aftershocks.

I don't give her time to recover.

I grab her by the hair and force her down. She goes down hard, knees hitting with a dull thud that makes her wince. But she doesn't protest. Just looks up at me with those wide, wrecked hazel eyes.

Fuck, she's beautiful like this. Destroyed. Mine.

"Open up, my little slut," I say, my voice rough, still breathless from fucking her so hard. I stroke my cock once, twice—still slick with her arousal, still rock-hard. "Time to have your cake and eat it too."

Her jaw drops instantly. No hesitation. No shame.

I shove my cock into her mouth before she can even take a breath. She gags immediately—throat convulsing around me as I push deeper, forcing her to take more than she's ready for. Her hands fly up to my thighs, nails digging into my flesh as she tries to steady herself, tries to breathe around the intrusion.

I keep going. Deeper. Until her nose is nearly pressed against my pelvis, until tears are streaming down her face and she's making these desperate, choking sounds that go straight to my balls.

Then—just when I feel her starting to panic, starting to push harder against my thighs—I pull out.

She gasps, coughing, sucking in air like she's been drowning. Her lips are swollen and wet and red. She looks utterly debauched.

I bend down and cup her face in both hands, tilting her head back, and I kiss her hard. Deep. Claiming her mouth the same way I just claimed her pussy.

I pour everything into that kiss—possession, obsession, the promise that this isn't over, that it will *never* be over.

She kisses me back—desperately, hungrily, like she needs my mouth more than air—and then her hand moves between us, finding my cock and wrapping around it with a grip so tight it borders on pain.

I pull back from the kiss with a sharp inhale, my entire body tensing as pleasure shoots through me like lightning. My head falls back, eyes squeezing shut, and I let out a low, guttural moan that I couldn't suppress if I tried.

"That's it," I rasp, forcing my eyes open to look down at her. "That's it, my good little slut. Fuck me with your hand."

She looks up at me with those wrecked, tear-streaked eyes, her hand still wrapped tight around my cock. Her grip is perfect—firm but not crushing, the pressure exactly where I need it.

"Please," she whispers, voice raw from choking on me. "Please, I need—put it back inside me. My pussy. Please, Master."

The word *Master* nearly breaks me. Seven months. Seven fucking months since I've heard that word from her lips.

I shake my head, grinning down at her. "No."

Her face crumples. "Please—"

"Open," I command, gripping her jaw. "Wider."

She obeys immediately, and I slide my cock back into that wet heat. This time I don't force it. Don't shove deep enough to make her gag. Instead I fist her hair—both hands tangled in all that platinum blonde—and use it to guide her head exactly how I want.

Back. Forward. Slow circles that make her lips stretch around my shaft.

"That's it," I breathe, watching my cock disappear between her swollen lips. "Fuck, that's perfect. You're so fucking good at this, baby."

She moans around me, the vibration traveling straight up my spine. Her tongue works the underside, tracing the vein that runs along my length, and I have to force myself not to thrust hard enough to make her choke again.

Not yet.

I want her to finish me properly this time. Want to feel her take control, show me what she can do when she's not fighting for air.

"Use your hand," I instruct, loosening my grip on her hair slightly. "Show me how well you know me."

Her hand comes up immediately, wrapping around the

base while her mouth works the head. The combination is devastating—wet heat and tight pressure in perfect rhythm. She hollows her cheeks, sucking hard, then releases to lap at the slit with the tip of her tongue.

"*Fuck*," I groan, head falling back. My hips start moving of their own accord, shallow thrusts that she matches perfectly.

She knows exactly what she's doing. Seven months hasn't dulled this at all. If anything, she's better—more confident, more deliberate. Like she's been fantasizing about this, practicing in her mind.

The thought makes my balls tighten.

"I'm close," I warn her, voice rougher than I intended. "You want to swallow me, baby? Want to taste it?"

Before I finish the question, she lunges forward.

Takes me deep—so fucking deep I feel the head hit the back of her throat. Her eyes water instantly but she doesn't pull back. Just holds there, throat convulsing around me, and then swallows.

The orgasm hits like a physical blow.

I come hard, buried in her throat, my entire body going rigid as pleasure detonates through me. Wave after wave, each pulse filling her mouth while she struggles to take it all.

I pull out before she chokes—before the lack of air becomes dangerous—and the last few spurts hit her face. Her cheek. Her lips. One thick rope across her nose.

I'm laughing before I can stop myself. Genuine laughter, rough and breathless, as I look down at her kneeling there covered in my come.

She's smiling too. Actually smiling, despite everything. Despite the tears and the way she's gasping for breath.

Fucking perfect.

I drop to my knees, cupping her face in both hands—not caring about the mess, not caring about anything except getting my mouth on hers. I kiss her hard. Brutal. Claiming every inch of that mouth.

Then soft. Gentle. Reverent, almost.

Then everything in between—rough, and tender, and possessive, and worshipful all at once. My tongue traces her bottom lip, tasting myself there, and I don't give a single fuck.

When I finally pull back, she's looking at me with those wide hazel eyes. Vulnerable. Open. Everything I've been craving for seven months.

"I love you," I say.

The words come out easier than I expected. No hesitation. No calculation. Just the truth, simple and absolute.

Her breath catches.

I stand before she can respond. Tuck myself back in, button and zip my pants. The fabric settles around my hips, and I'm already moving toward the door.

"Caleb—"

"You know where to find me," I say without turning around. My hand finds the doorknob. "When you're ready."

I open the door.

Walk through.

Close it behind me with a soft click that sounds impossibly loud in the silence.

Then I'm in the hallway, walking toward the stairs, my heart pounding so hard I can feel it in my throat.

I didn't lie.

I won't come back.

Not until she comes to me first.

The thought terrifies me more than anything I've ever done.

But she *will* come.

I've already made sure of it.

CHAPTER 13
SCARLETTA

The cost of being thoroughly fucked twice by two dominant men in the same day is a pussy so sore, I can still feel their phantom cocks inside me the next morning—which came after zero minutes of sleep.

And… I'm there again.

First with Ryan fucking me on that table set up between tripods that were definitely meant to film porn. Ankles strapped in to stirrups as he pounded me. The look on his face was… what?

Definitely pleasure.

But there was something more there.

Something almost boyish in the way he was discovering me.

Then Caleb. Psycho stalker sitting in the shadows like a freak.

How long was he waiting in my apartment? I have no idea. There's no security system in this place. I might need one though. If I want to keep him away.

Do… I want to keep him away?

Caleb is way more complicated than Ryan. Gym owner using clients to make porn? It's dark and nasty, but hundreds of levels above the sickness of being aroused by killing someone.

The look on Caleb's face that day in the maze as he tortured that man. It was pure, raw lust radiating from him. His cock was rock-hard the entire time.

I was too confused and terrified to fully process shit. My mind was scrambling, desperately trying to make sense of what the hell was happening.

Everything felt surreal.

But I saw his hard cock swinging between his legs like a fucking sausage. Was like… zeroed in on it.

And the way he came on the bloody body—I'll never forget that.

That final image will be burned into my brain forever.

That's not even the sickest thing, either.

I close my eyes, shaking my head as I try not to think about this. I don't want to think about this…

But… I was aroused too.

Oh, god.

There, I said it. I admitted it. The sight of Caleb killing that man after he hurt me. How hard he was. How hard he came. How his come spurted out like a fucking eruption.

I came too.

It's so sick. So fucking sick. My fingers were between my legs as I watched and… I didn't even realize it.

I did exactly what Caleb did.

I am just like him.

I am sick.

Even now, lying here in these rumpled sheets at four in the morning, staring at the ceiling in the dark with absolutely zero sleep and my mind running this endless, spiraling speedrun through every horrific detail—I'm wet.

My pussy is throbbing.

Just like it always is when I remember.

Until now, though, I've been pushing away the truth.

That's why I didn't masturbate until this past week.

I couldn't get past the idea that I'm a sick fuck just like Caleb.

That's why he needs to go away.

It's not because I don't like him.

It's because I like him too much.

Ryan is… maybe not normal. But I'm not looking for normal. I'm looking for… well, his kind of freak flag is something I can deal with. Something I can get on board with.

Strapping me into gyno contraptions? Yes. Yes. I'm here for it. It's actually a common thread in my recent sex history.

Practically vanilla at this point.

I might even let him film me. With a mask on. Maybe. The thought sends a sharp pulse of heat straight through me— imagining strangers watching, their eyes glued to the screen, their hands working themselves into a frenzy over *me*. Over what I'm doing. What I'm letting Ryan do to me.

It's twisted and exhibitionistic and exactly the kind of thing that should make me feel ashamed, but instead I'm just… turned on. Picturing some faceless person on the other side of a computer screen, jerking off to footage of me strapped into that contraption, spread open and vulnerable and *wanting* it.

Using what they see as fuel for their own fantasies, their own future encounters. Planning out scenarios with their partners based on what they watched me experience with Ryan.

The idea shouldn't be hot.

But it is.

This is my justification—my permission, my excuse, whatever I need to call it to make it okay—when my hand slowly lowers, fingertips trailing down my stomach, hesitating at my hip bone before sliding further. Ryan. The cameras. The knowledge that someone might be watching this exact moment, cataloging it for later use. That's what I tell myself this is about.

I picture it. Ryan's hands on my ankles, lifting them, positioning them exactly where he wants them. The cold metal stirrups against my calves as he locks them in. That click. The finality of it.

I'm already touching myself, fingers sliding through the wetness that's been building all night.

In my mind, I'm spread wide on that table. Exposed. The cameras positioned at deliberate angles—one overhead, one between my legs, one capturing my face. Ryan stepping back to check the framing. Adjusting the ring lights so there's no shadow obscuring anything important.

He'd make me wait. Test me. Let me lie there with my pussy on display while he fucks around with settings and equipment, taking his time, letting the anticipation build until I'm squirming against the restraints.

My fingers circle my clit, pressure building as I imagine him finally approaching. Standing between my spread thighs. The bulge in his joggers right there, eye level if I could lift my head.

"You ready to be famous, button?"

I whimper into my empty apartment, hips lifting off the mattress.

The fantasy Ryan doesn't ask permission. He just pulls his cock out—thick and heavy—and drags the head through my folds. Teasing. Making me beg for it while the cameras record everything.

"Please," I whisper to no one, fingers working faster. "Please fuck me."

Fantasy Ryan grips my hips and slams inside in one brutal thrust. No warning. No gentleness. Just claiming what's his while the cameras capture every second.

He fucks me hard on that table, using the stirrups as leverage to drive deeper. Each thrust punches the air from my lungs. The restraints dig into my ankles. I'm completely helpless, completely his, and everyone watching will know it.

"That's it, button. Show them what a dirty little slut you are."

My fingers move frantically now, circling my clit while I imagine him pounding into me. The wet sounds. The slap of skin. His grunts mixing with my moans. All of it recorded. Permanent. Evidence of exactly how much I need this.

"Come for the camera," fantasy Ryan commands. "Let them see."

And I do. I come so fucking hard my back arches off the mattress, thighs trembling, a scream tearing from my throat that echoes through my empty apartment. Wave after wave crashes through me while I work myself through it, imagining those cameras capturing every spasm, every desperate sound.

When I finally collapse back onto the bed, panting and limp, I'm staring at the ceiling again.

My pussy is still throbbing.

Why am I such a freak?

It could be worse, inner monologue reasons. *You could be coming to the image of Caleb killing someone…*

I throw the sheet off me and get out of bed. I'm not thinking about him.

Caleb is over.

I want Ryan.

I need Ryan.

Ryan, with his cute porn obsession. Ryan with his tame camera set up. Ryan with his button nick name.

I mean, little button?

Or good little slut?

The choice is obvious.

I note the time as I get in the shower. I've got forty-five minutes before I have to meet Ryan at the Gym.

I'm going to let him film me.

Maybe I won't even ask for a mask.

The gym is open when I get there. People come early. People who work real jobs and have real daytime schedules. But it's only about a half a dozen.

Ryan's fishbowl office upstairs is dark. Which is weird. We've been meeting here at five AM for training for nearly two weeks now and that office has never been dark when I came in.

Maybe he's already in the back setting up?

I walk down the hallway to the big double doors that lead into the empty space where the cameras are, pull on the handle and… it's locked.

I knock. "Ryan? Are you in there?"

Nothing.

I put my ear against the cold metal. Knock again. "Ryan?"

Silence.

OK. Well. He's not here yet.

I check my phone. It's only five oh three.

So I go back out to the gym, casually saying hi to people who wave and smile at me. I'm a regular here. I fit in.

I like that.

I get on one of the treadmills and put my ear buds in. I'll warm up while I wait.

Twenty minutes later I realize… he's not coming.

Twenty-one minutes later, I understand why.

Caleb.

He came to me last night so that when I got here and found Ryan missing, I'd know.

He's jealous.

And when a man who literally gets off on murder gets jealous, how else does this end?

He's going to kill him.

That sick fuck is going to kill Ryan just because I chose him.

I'm shaking as I leave the gym and walk home. When I get there, I search around in my purse for the card. The business card Caleb gave me weeks ago after he paid that Marty guy to talk dirty to me on our date.

You know where to find me…

Yes, Caleb, I *do* know where to find you.

In a log mansion outside of Jackson Hole.

I grab my keys and walk out, slamming the door behind me.

He's not gonna get away with this.

He doesn't get to decide my future.

And if he's laid a single finger on Ryan—if he's done anything to him, anything at all, if he's hurt him, or threatened him, or made him disappear—I swear to God, I'll kill him myself.

I'll find a way.

I don't care how big he is, how strong, how prepared.

I don't care about his security, or his money, or his power.

I'll make him pay for this.

The moment this thought appears, I'm wet again. Pussy throbbing. I'm seeing Caleb's swinging dick again. The way he came on that man in the maze. The way I came watching.

"*No,*" I growl, clicking my key fob to unlock my Jeep door.

I do not get off on murder.

That's *his* kink, not mine.

Not mine, not mine, not mine…

I chant this inside my head as I pull out of the parking garage and head east…

CHAPTER 14
CALEB

The sun is just beginning to rise above the tree line outside my log mansion. Backlit mountains capped by the perfect spread of roiling cloud cover turns the entire landscape into a surreal mixture of colors.

Green grass and trees, peppered by the darker browns of wood.

Pink, orange, coral, purple sky.

And a feeling in the air that today is important.

If I were the kind of man who brags about his highlights on 'hashtag mountain life' like an entitled asshole, this golden-hour photo op would get attention.

Spoiler alert: I'm not.

So I'm the only one who will ever know this moment existed.

The story of my life, perhaps.

I'm thinking about Ryan Adamson's security setup. A completely unnecessary kind of overkill that shouldn't be in a small-town gym unless you're hiding something… *interesting.*

Encrypted camera feeds that didn't just resist my initial probes—they actively told me to fuck off.

Physical access controls better than some banks I've robbed.

Network architecture that screams "I paid a professional who knows what actual threats look like."

Your average gym bro doesn't know the difference between WPA2 and WPA3, let alone implement air-gapped systems.

But Ryan built a fortress around Iron River Fitness. The kind of fortress that makes a man wonder what exactly requires that level of protection.

Trade secrets for revolutionary TRX modifications?

Client privacy for Idaho Falls' moderately affluent fitness enthusiasts?

No. That's not what our boy Ryan here needs the security for.

I take a sip of the lukewarm coffee, then set the mug down and touch my sternum where Scarletta's face is inked on the skin—the throat-fucking scene Posie inked, years before I ever met her.

Stella Six Feather's recollection of 'the psychopath with the bird tattoos' was all I had.

Turns out, it was all I needed.

Stella came right out and said that Ryan killed Posie. No hesitation at all.

It's a ridiculous claim. Not to be trusted. I like Stella. That final, fourth CNC she did for the auction house was chef's fucking kiss. She agreed to everything—for bonuses, obviously. A literal gang rape courtesy of European princes and dukes. Earls and barons. Marquess and viscounts.

But that's still the number one film requested by members when they come to stay at the Cheyenne Club. It's been number one for years.

Stella has no idea how famous she is.

No idea that celebrities worldwide come to her little Jackson Hole tattoo parlor because of it.

Not that she wouldn't be successful without that fame, she would. She's good. But it never hurts to have the global rich and powerful dying to book an appointment in your shop so they can see you in person after watching you take a royal cock in the pussy, in the ass, and down the throat at the same time.

The point is, to Stella, Ryan had a vibe.

Which made me wonder, what was the vibe she got off of me?

I didn't ask, she had no trouble recalling the work Posie did for me. When I walk into a tattoo shop and take off my shirt, *everyone* notices. That's why I don't let any artist do more than one.

Our boy, Ryan, though? He either didn't think that one through—unlikely. Or he enjoys the attention. Ding, ding, ding.

Birds, though. I can see why he took the risk. It feels safe.

But there are two kinds of people who cover their body in skin art.

The randos and the collectors.

Randos are just that. *I think I'll get a tattoo today. Maybe a Tasmanian Devil?*

But collectors have a theme. *I'm inking up my body with symbols that represent ME.*

So by default, Ryan was a collector.

Which means the artist takes note.

What do the birds mean to Ryan?

Perhaps I'll ask before I kill him.

Because I *am* going to kill him.

But it wasn't the tattoos, or Stella's claim that made me come to this conclusion. It was Scarletta.

Of course, it was Scarletta. I can't be certain that what she told me last night was the truth. *He pushed his finger into my mouth. Just shoved it in like I was a whore. And I came. Right there. Fully clothed. Just from his finger. He spread me wide open.*

Bound. Helpless. Exactly the way I like it. And then he fucked me so hard I felt it for hours afterward. He came all over me. Marked me. Told me to come back tomorrow morning at five AM for round two.

My cock is throbbing. This is what she does to me. The absolute way Scarletta Mae Desmond hijacks my attention should be infuriating.

But it's not.

It just makes me want her more.

Makes me want to possess her.

Makes me want to lock her in a room where only I exist. Where my voice is the only sound. My hands the only touch. My approval the only currency that matters.

I want to crawl inside her skull and live there. Set up permanent residence in the space between her thoughts and her shame. I want to know every fantasy before she finishes thinking it. Every fear before it fully forms.

I want her so completely that the concept of "Scarletta without Caleb" becomes linguistically impossible. A grammatical error. A failure of basic logic.

This is what normal men don't understand.

They think possession means ownership. Legal titles. Marriage certificates. Joint bank accounts.

Idiots.

Possession means she can't come without thinking of me. Can't write a sentence without wondering if I'll read it. Can't look at herself in the mirror without seeing what I see.

It means her body responds to my voice before her brain catches up.

It means when she touches herself at four in the morning, it's my face she's imagining.

My cock.

My control.

Not Ryan fucking Adamson's.

He's not her Helix.

I'm her Helix. I'm the monster in the maze with the dark she hungers for.

I'm the creature that haunts her wettest dreams.

I'm all her shameful sexual fantasies come true.

Me.

Not him.

We are not the same.

And now… I will prove it.

The late morning August heat swarms around me. A living, oppressive cloak. The insects in the Tetons this time of year are absolutely insane—mosquitoes the size of quarters, biting flies that draw blood, gnats that swarm in clouds so dense they fill your mouth if you're stupid enough to breathe through it.

It's enough to make a person swear off nature forever, pack up their Gore-Tex and their romanticized notions of wilderness solitude, and retreat to climate-controlled civilization where the only bugs are the occasional cockroach you can crush with your shoe.

But to those of us who actually belong here—who understand that nature isn't a postcard or a wellness retreat, but something ancient and indifferent—it's a minor inconvenience.

An annoyance to be endured with the same patience you'd give to traffic or a tedious board meeting.

You learn to adapt and prepare. Long sleeves even in eighty-degree heat, long pants tucked into your boots like you're dressing for a tick-borne plague. You keep leather work gloves and a wide-brimmed hat with mosquito netting in the back of your Jeep, along with the industrial-strength DEET that probably causes cancer, but definitely prevents you from being eaten alive.

It's the price of admission to this particular cathedral, and you pay it without hesitation because the alternative—soft skin exposed to the wilderness—marks you as prey rather than predator.

You accept that the mountains take their pound of flesh in sweat and blood and itching welts, and you pay it without complaint.

For young men tied to posts and left overnight, however —naked and immobilized, unable to swat, or scratch, or shield themselves from the relentless assault of a thousand tiny mandibles—it's considerably more than inconvenient.

It's torture.

Well. Mild torture. Torture-adjacent, let's call it.

The path from the house to the clearing is about a quarter of a mile of dense forest. It's mostly a deer trail. Some places, it disappears all together. Becoming something to be felt, rather than followed.

Ryan Adamson is right where I left him yesterday afternoon. Sitting down against a tree trunk shoulders cranked behind his back, wrists held together with nylon rope.

Even if I left him clothed, he would still look like this.

Covered in spots of blood, welts, and looking like he lost his mind about ten hours ago.

He should consider himself lucky. Last spring there was a wolf pack up here. A pack that became accustomed to being fed human flesh from this very post. But territory boundaries have changed over the summer, so I guess our boy Ryan here got a pass on being eaten alive.

At least, in that sense.

When I approach, he looks up at me with that dazed, confused stare one only finds on statues of the Crucifixion of Jesus Christ. Eyes rolled back, vacant mind, suffering evident.

He doesn't beg. Or even try to talk when I bend down and untie him. And once he's unsecured, he falls over sideways.

I pull the sawed-off shotgun from my hip and point it at him. "If you think I'm going to carry you, you're mistaken. Would you like a chance to save your life? Or should I blow your head off right here?"

It's a true Helix moment for me. Because it's a lie.

Ryan's head wobbles as he tries to find my face. His eyes squint, trying to see me properly through the backlighting. But he doesn't answer.

"Do you have any idea how quickly ants would consume your body out here? How quickly they could strip the flesh from your bones?"

Still, he says nothing. Just continues giving me the old Jesus-Christ-Superstar look.

"Ask me how I know this, Ryan."

"Who..." his throat is so dry, he can barely speak. "Who the fuck sent you? Huh? What do you want? Money? Is it money? Did Larson send you? Was it Larson? I told that fucker, I've got his girl. She's lined up for next month. These things take planning. You understand, right?"

I nod. Solemn. Because I actually do.

Ryan takes this nod as affirmation. "So it *is* Larson? *Fuck.* What the fuck? Why is he such a psychopath?" He narrows his eyes at me. "You gonna tell him I said that?"

I cross my arms, shake my head, and press my lips together. "I don't even know who fuckin' Larson is."

"*What?*" Ryan's brows get so crinkled, they practically touch in the middle. "You just said—"

"No, *you* just said. I just agreed that I do understand how these things go. In a way. In a very specific way that doesn't involve anything of the kind of what you actually do."

"What the hell does *that* mean?"

I'm holding the sawed-off with one hand as I bend down, take a fistful of his hair in the other, and press the barrel against his chest. "It means that I absolutely understand how hard it is to find suitable candidates for one's… *hobby*. Except, it's not a hobby for you, is it Ryan? It's a business."

I yank on his hair as I stand. Forcing him to scramble to stand with me. Then I push him out in front of me and say, "Walk. Follow the trail."

He doesn't.

He's not used to this. The loss of control. It's new to him. He just stands there, looking at me with his fish-mouth gaping, trying to work out what the actual fuck is happening right now.

He'll never work it out. He so far behind. I'm running a masterclass in predator-prey dynamics and he still thinks this has got something to do with an order some Larson guy put in for a girl next month.

Obviously, that's not what this is about.

So I pull the trigger.

The shotgun round blasts out the twelve-inch barrel with a deafening crack that echoes through the trees, and the trunk of a pine just to the left of Ryan's shoulder explodes in a spray of bark and splinters. Wood fragments pepper his face. He flinches—finally—stumbling sideways with his hands up like that'll stop the next one.

I tilt my head at Ryan Adamson as I rack the sawed-off. Curious. What is going through that head of his right now? "Do I need to ask you again?"

He shakes out a no answer, then turns. His bare feet stumbling on the path as he limps forward. His fingertips automatically scratching the bloody bites all over his naked body.

Ryan proceeds, his naked body weaving between trees as I chuckle when his feet catch on roots and rocks. I watch him flinch when branches scrape his insect-ravaged skin. Enjoying it.

I'm already planning how he dies.

Slow. Obviously. But not elaborate.

The barn will do fine. Concrete floor. Drain. Hose. The cameras are already installed—six angles, motion-activated, cloud backup. I'll record everything. Archive it. Maybe I'll watch it later when I'm thinking about Scarletta and need something to push me over the edge.

My cock thickens against my zipper.

I picture Ryan strung up from the ceiling beam. Bleeding out slowly while I explain exactly what he did wrong. While I describe in graphic detail what Scarletta looks like when she comes.

How she whimpers *my* name, not his.

How I am her Helix, not him.

I reach down and adjust myself through my jeans, feeling the unmistakable throb of arousal. The denim constrains my partial erection, forcing me to shift my grip on the shotgun as I palm myself briefly.

The trees thin ahead. My cabin materializes through the pines. The barn squats beside it, utterly unremarkable from the outside if you don't look close.

But on the inside—which is clearly visible now, I made damn sure of it, left both barn doors thrown wide open—there's a gambrel and two industrial meat hooks dangling from the ceiling.

It hangs from heavy-gauge chain looped through the rafters. The chain connects to an electric hoist mounted on the beam above. The kind of equipment you'd use on a farm to hoist a slaughtered pig by its hind legs, suspend the carcass at working height for scalding and gutting.

The kind that can lift eight hundred pounds without breaking a sweat.

It's overkill for this situation. But... that's me. Mr. Overkill.

Ryan stops at the barn entrance. His shoulders tense. His head tilts slightly as he registers the gambrel, the hooks, the concrete floor with the drain centered beneath the hoist.

I watch the understanding ripple through his body. The

way his breathing changes. The instinctive half-step backward before he catches himself.

I nudge the shotgun barrel between his shoulder blades. "Keep moving."

The sound hits me before I process it. Gravel crunching under tires. Engine noise climbing the access road.

My head snaps toward the driveway. The black Jeep comes up the hill like a speed demon, dust trailing behind it like a contrail, then skids to a stop, spraying gravel.

Scarletta? What the fuck is she doing here? How did she even—

Ryan moves.

His elbow drives into my throat with force. My vision whites out. The pain is immediate and blinding. His hand clamps around the shotgun barrel, shoving it wide as my finger involuntarily contracts on the trigger.

The blast tears through the barn wall. Splinters explode outward. The recoil rips the weapon from my grip and it skitters across the concrete, tumbling end over end until it slides out into the driveway.

We hit the ground together. Hard. My skull cracks against concrete and the world tilts sideways.

Ryan's weight crashes down on top of me with the full force of his body. His hips shift immediately—not wild thrashing, not desperate scrambling. Deliberate and controlled. The kind of precision that comes from muscle memory so deep it bypasses conscious thought.

His legs snake around my torso in a fluid motion, pulling guard with textbook efficiency. His thighs lock tight across my ribs as he fights for dominant position, every micro-adjustment executed with the kind of technical mastery you only acquire after thousands of hours on the mat.

Twelve hours tied to a tree covered in insect bites doesn't erase muscle memory, and the way he moves tells me everything I should've known, but didn't.

Brazilian Ju-jitsu.

I try to buck him off but he's already transitioned. His arm slides under my chin. The other threads behind my head. His forearm presses against my carotid artery like he's done this thousands of times.

Rear naked choke.

The pressure builds immediately. My vision narrows at the edges. I claw at his arm but he's locked in tight. Hips controlled. Weight distributed perfectly.

Ryan's breath is hot against my ear. "Who the fuck sent you?"

I can't answer. Can't breathe. The world is going grey.

He's screaming now. "*Who the fuck sent you!*"

But he still doesn't understand.

It's this realization that pisses me off.

Not the fact that he got me. That he's winning. That I messed up—again—all because I was too distracted by Scarletta Mae Desmond to thoroughly check out my prey.

It's the lack of clarity.

You can't balance the scales if your prey doesn't understand *why*.

Everything goes black.

CHAPTER 15
SCARLETTA

The fucking asshole.

Caleb MacLeay is a controlling, motherfucking asshole.

Two hours of switchbacks and my knuckles are white, my nerves are frazzled, and cursing Caleb MacLeay's name and damning him to hell is the only way I know to process this fucking drive.

I am not cut out for this. There's a reason I stay on my side of the fucking Tetons! They're sketchy, and twisty, and fucking elk and moose are trying to throw themselves in front of my Jeep at every switchback.

And what's waiting for me at the end of my Teton Pass struggle session?

Who the fuck knows? A dead body? Some crazy torture session? Nothing, because he's not even here?

Could be any of those.

Torture… I picture how he killed that Russian man on the island.

Oh god. My foot presses down on the accelerator, speeding up on the dirt road, when the navigation says, "Turn left now."

What? I slam on the brakes, twist the wheel to the left, and

Tokyo Drift my way under a ranch archway marked with a skull and crossbones.

I'm here.

I accelerate again as I climb the steep driveway. Towering pines thick enough to get lost in blur by, all caution for elk and moose out the window.

Caleb's log mansion materializes through the trees. A tower of timber and glass, it's perched on the mountainside like some psychopath's wet dream of isolation and control.

I slam on the brakes again, this time kicking up a cloud of gravel and dust between the house and the barn.

"You have arrived at your destination."

I take a deep breath. Yeah. I sure the fuck have.

I get out of the car and immediately, I'm confronted with the sound of something exploding. For a moment, I'm just stunned, processing. *Frozen.*

Then I hear grunting, and panting, and… what the fuck is happening?

"Who sent you? *Who the fuck sent you!*" The yell echos through the trees.

"Ryan?" I scream. Then I'm running. This stupidity of this doesn't hit me until I'm at the threshold to the barn. Why am I running towards this? What the hell is wrong with me?

Because there they are! On the ground. Fighting. Ryan is naked and covered in—I have no idea. Blood. Splotches of it cover his whole body, smudging his bird tattoos as he and Caleb twist and grapple on the concrete.

This is when I see the shotgun at my feet. It's very short. Very illegal. Very much a signal that whatever is happening here is *bad, bad, bad.*

That's what that noise was. Not an explosion, a shotgun.

My fingers wrap around the stock before my brain catches up to my body.

What am I doing? What the fuck am I doing?

But I'm already lifting it. Already feeling the weight of it—

heavier than I expected, the metal still warm from being fired. The smell hits me next. Gunpowder. Sharp, and acrid, and *real* in a way that makes my stomach lurch.

I've written this. I've written this exact moment a dozen times. The heroine finds the weapon. The heroine takes control.

But I'm not a heroine. I'm a fucking mess in yoga pants who drove two hours to confront a murderer and now there's *two* men covered in blood and I don't know which one is the monster anymore.

Rack it. You have to rack it.

The thought comes from somewhere outside myself. From every action movie I've ever watched. From the scene in *Captive Hearts* where Lydia disarms her kidnapper. From muscle memory that doesn't belong to me—that belongs to characters I invented, women who were braver than I'll ever be.

My hands move.

Chk-chk.

The sound is obscene. Mechanical. Final.

Both men freeze.

The fighting stops like someone hit pause on a video. Ryan's arm is locked around Caleb's throat. Caleb's face is red, his eyes bulging, but now they're both staring at me.

At the gun in my shaking hands.

Oh god. Oh god oh god oh god.

I'm pointing it at them. At *both* of them. The barrel swings from Caleb to Ryan and back again because I don't know—I don't fucking *know*—

"Don't move." My voice comes out wrong. Too high. Cracking on the second word like a teenager's. "Don't fucking move."

Ryan's grip on Caleb loosens slightly. His eyes—they're calculating. Reading me. Seeing exactly how terrified I am.

He knows I don't know what I'm doing.

"Either of you." I force the words out louder. Swing the barrel back toward Caleb, then Ryan, then somewhere in between. "Don't. Fucking. *Move*."

My arms are trembling. The gun is too heavy. I can feel my pulse in my fingertips, in my throat, behind my eyes.

I'm going to throw up.

I'm going to drop this gun.

I'm going to get us all killed.

You're not in your stories anymore, Scarletta. This is real. This is fucking real.

Ryan starts first. "Do you know this guy?"

And as he says this, Caleb gets free, he's on his feet, reaching for Ryan—

The shotgun goes off.

The sound is *enormous*—a physical thing that slaps me across the face, makes my ears ring, rattles my teeth in my skull. The recoil slams into my stomach hard enough that I stagger back a step, almost drop the damn thing.

Splinters of wood rain down from above.

Oh god. Oh shit. Oh fuck.

I didn't mean to—or did I? My finger pulled the trigger. The gun fired. There's a hole in the roof now, a ragged circle of daylight punching through the shadows, dust motes swirling in the sudden beam of summer sun.

Both men freeze.

Caleb's hand is still reaching for Ryan. Ryan's mouth is open mid-word. They're both staring at me with identical expressions—shock, maybe fear, definitely a recalculation of how dangerous I actually am.

Good.

"I SAID—" My voice cracks again but I push through it, louder, shriller, channeling every ounce of hysteria clawing up my throat. "*DON'T. FUCKING. MOVE!*"

I rack the shotgun again.

The sound is satisfying in a way I don't have time to

examine—that heavy *ka-CHUNK* of metal sliding, a shell ejecting, another one chambering. Both men's hands shoot up immediately. Palms out. Fingers spread. Universal gesture of surrender.

They're listening now.

My stomach throbs where the stock hit it. My ears are still ringing. The gun is too heavy, my arms are shaking worse than before, and I think I bit my tongue because I can taste blood.

But they're not moving.

They're not fucking *moving*.

Ryan continues. "He kidnapped me! Fucking kidnapped me!" He sounds scared. But he should be. He's naked, covered in what I can now determine to be… bug bites? And he understands, somehow, what Caleb is about to do to him.

Was.

Until I showed up.

"Scarletta…" Caleb is cool. One-hundred percent in control. "You have no idea who he is. Ask him what he had planned for you at five am this morning. Ask him."

Ryan looks at Caleb like… like he's… I don't even understand that look.

But I feel it. "How did you know I was meeting him at five am?"

"Ask him, Scarletta," Caleb repeats. Then he spits on the ground. Blood. "Ask him what his real business is. Not the gym, Scar. The real business. Ask him who the fuck Posie Little is."

Ryan's whole face goes white.

I don't know what this is about, but whatever it is, Caleb should not have this information. Because that look on Ryan's face is… panic.

Caleb laughs. Rips off his long-sleeve black henley. And there they are. All those tattoos. All those psycho tattoos of me being fucked, and dominated, and humiliated by him. My face, all over his body.

"What the fuck is this?" Ryan asks. But he's unsure now. Past angry, past confused. He looks at me. Looks back at Caleb. Then me again. "Is that your face?"

I don't have time to answer because Caleb's already talking."Posie Little did this tattoo for me." He points to the one over his sternum where he's throat-fucking me. He looks at Ryan. "Just the one. Because unlike you, I'm not stupid enough to use the same artist twice. How does it feel, *Ryan*, to know that it was those fucking birds on your body that signed your death certificate?"

"What are you talking about?" I'm breathless. Barely able to take in air. Something big is happening right now, I just don't understand what it is.

All I know is... it's bad.

"Posie did all those bird tattoos on GymBro here," Caleb says. "Died under suspicious circumstances a while back." His voice is eerily calm. A complete disconnect with what I'm feeling.

"Scarletta," Ryan says, his voice filled with building panic. "Don't listen to him. He has no idea what he's talking about."

I'm so confused. I don't understand what a tattoo artist has to do with anything.

"Don't I?" Caleb asks. "Don't I, Ryan? Let's fill in some blanks, shall we? Iron River Fitness has crazy security. You know my set up, Scar. You've seen it. You know I understand surveillance."

I nod, blankly. Just because he's right. This is something I've seen first hand.

"I wasn't even looking for Ryan here when I hacked into the Bonneville County IT system. Just the coroner report for Posie. Just curious, that's all. Posie's autopsy report was suspiciously brief. The tox screen didn't match her clean history. Unexplained bruising, vocal cords shredded."

I'm looking at his tattoo when he says this. The one where he's throat fucking me. The one Posie did.

"But it wasn't just Posie," Caleb continues. "Many young women dead over the past three years. All ruled accidental or OD. Cases were all closed fast. And the coroner's financials don't match his salary. He's got a new truck. A new boat. Cash deposits weekly."

"Scarletta," Ryan interjects again. "Whatever this is about, he's lying."

Caleb doesn't bother replying to him. Just continues. "They run Windows 7 on a shared network. Sheriff, coroner, county clerk. They're all connected. I had an AI agent do a simple search for me and guess what I found?"

"Lies," Ryan snarls. "This is all lies."

But I don't think it is. And Caleb is looking me dead in the eyes right now. "You were going to meet him at five AM?"

I'm nodding out a yes, as Ryan continues to protest. But I'm not even listening to Ryan. I'm watching Caleb's face go sad.

Not angry.

Sad.

"You know what an onion address looks like now, right Scarletta? I showed you how to access the site I use for the auction."

The dark web. He's talking about the dark web and how I used that long string of numbers to get to his site.

"Auction? What the fuck is he talking about?" Ryan is losing his shit.

"Well, I found an address like that in an email chain between Ryan and a deputy. Only it didn't lead to an auction house."

I'm going to be sick. "Where did it go?"

"A snuff film site. Custom orders—"

"Lies!" Ryan screams.

"I found a calendar of upcoming productions."

"You found nothing," Ryan screams. "Scarletta, this man is a psychopath! He fucking kidnapped me! Took my clothes! Left me outside all night tied to a tree! Look at me! Look at all the bites on me! He was going to hang me from that chain. Look! Look up!"

I do look up. I see the chain. The hooks. Can perfectly imagine what Caleb was gonna do to Ryan. Like... *every* bit of it. Because I've seen him in action.

But it doesn't matter, Caleb is talking. "This morning, Scarletta. The next film was going to be this morning starting at five AM Mountain Time. A live event featuring a platinum blonde, fitness enthusiast."

He was going to kill me.

Kill me.

Kill.

Me.

Ryan was gonna turn those cameras on, put me on that table, strap me in, and... what? Torture me?

On film.

Then kill me to fulfill an order.

An order.

A snuff film.

I look at Ryan. The shotgun looks too.

And suddenly, everything about my life becomes crystal clear.

Time slows down.

Stops.

And I'm in that place between here and there where nothing exists but my mind.

My beautiful, fucked-up, pitch-black mind.

Lyra. Poor Lyra. Plucked from her life without consent. Abducted by Helix and dragged into his dark, subterranean world. Claiming she's his destined mate, but she must first prove herself capable of surviving his brutal realm. Before their union can occur, she must face

The Labyrinth—an ancient trial that determines worthiness.

Helix tells Lyra that a portal to her world waits at the maze's center. If she reaches it, she can return home. This is a lie. No portal exists. She's trapped in his world permanently.

The only question really is, will she be able to live with herself in the end?

Lyra enters the maze alone, pursued by three animalistic monsters—Helix's enemies who view human females as breeding stock. If caught, she faces rape, captivity, and repeated sexual violation as a slave-breeder.

Helix's voice guides her via telepathic bond through shortcuts and portal-jumps. She must trust his instructions completely despite survival instincts screaming otherwise.

Despite his help, she is captured three times. Tackled and pinned. Dragged toward a breeding chamber. Restrained and violated.

Lyra reaches the center broken, discovering no portal exists. Helix awaits to "heal" and claim her—the lesser evil, but still captivity.

She falls into his arms.

Grateful.

Trigger Warnings:
  Forced Proximity
  Non Consent/Rape
  Ravished by monsters that resemble animals
  Trauma Bonding
  Stockholm Syndrome
  Abduction/Kidnapping
  Captivity/Imprisonment
  Breeding Kink
  Multiple Attackers
  Deception/Manipulation by Love Interest

False Hope/Psychological Cruelty
Chase/Hunt Dynamics
Telepathic Invasion/Mind Intrusion
Forced Mating/Claiming
Monster Romance (Non-Human MMC)
Dubious Consent with "Hero"
No True Escape
Gaslighting as Romance
Prey/Predator Dynamics
Graphic Sexual Violence
Choosing the "Lesser Monster" as HEA
Dark HEA (not safe, not healthy, not conventional)
Heroine Breaks Before Surrender
No Redemption Arc
The Monster Wins

This is my life. It's built on nothing but a list of the most fucked-up trigger warnings.

And it's... just... who I am.

What can I say?

I wrote that story. I loved that story. I wanted to live that story. Wanted it so much, I walked into a copy of that maze on Caleb's island, ready to allow three attackers to have their way with me before finding my Helix at the center.

I did that willingly.

Craved it.

This is what sexually satisfies me.

This darkness is who I am.

This is the truth of my situation. The things I want—the thing *I am*—draws predators. That's why Derek raped me. I summoned him to me because I wanted what he was offering and he saw it. Somehow, he knew.

That Russian man in the maze. My second attacker. I don't know how to explain that one. I have no idea what that was.

But the reason he got me? Yes, I do understand that. He got me because I was *there*. Getting off on weird kink.

And now… Ryan.

He doesn't make porn. He makes snuff films. And something about me told him that I was a candidate.

Who are you kidding, Scarletta? You told him you were a candidate. You practically begged him to strap your ankles into stirrups and fuck you blind.

If I want to run the maze, I have to deal with the monsters.

This is the truth of my sickness.

Helix kidnapped Lyra. He made her run the maze to prove she could survive it. Then he became the monster she could live with.

The darkness she could survive.

I look at Caleb. His eyes are still sad. "Are you OK?"

I don't answer, just look at Ryan. He's in full panic mode. He's been talking this whole time. Excuse after excuse. Lie after lie spewing from his mouth.

He was going to kill me.

He goes silent.

We lock eyes.

His change. Right in front of me.

And there he is.

The predator.

The killer.

The monster I never saw coming.

He lunges, and I don't even blink.

I pull the trigger and the next thing I know, he's meat.

CHAPTER 16
CALEB

The shotgun kicks against Scarletta's stomach.

Ryan's chest opens like a flower blooming in reverse—red petals spraying outward, wet and immediate. The force throws him backward, and what hits the concrete floor isn't a person anymore. Just meat and bone and the copper-bright smell of fresh death.

I watch Scarletta.

Not the body. Not the spreading pool beneath what used to be Ryan Adamson.

Her.

Blood mists her face in a fine spray. Droplets cling to her platinum hair like scattered rubies, catching the barn's dim light. Across her forearms, streaks of crimson where the blowback painted her skin. Her chest heaves, breath coming in sharp, ragged gasps that make her whole body shudder.

There's blood on her lip.

A single dark smear, almost black against the pink.

She's hyperventilating now, hands shaking so violently the shotgun rattles. She drops it—the clatter against concrete sounds distant, irrelevant. Her fingers come up to her face, swiping at the blood, but she's only smearing it. Spreading

Ryan across her cheeks, her chin, her forehead. She spits, tries to clear her mouth, and the motion just transfers more of him onto her tongue.

She's panicking.

And I'm hard.

Fully, achingly erect. The kind that strains against fabric and demands attention.

I should be concerned about the body. The cleanup. The evidence. The fact that she just committed murder in my barn, and her fingerprints are all over the weapon, and this will require significant resources to make disappear.

Instead, I'm watching blood drip from her jawline onto her collarbone, and my cock throbs like it has its own heartbeat.

She's the most beautiful thing I've ever seen.

I take a step toward her, and my hand moves without conscious decision—sliding down, between my waistband and my skin, wrapping around my cock.

Her gaze drops to my hand. To what I'm doing.

The horror in her expression should stop me.

It doesn't.

This is wrong. I understand that intellectually. A man lies dead three feet away, and I'm stroking myself while his blood dries on the face of the woman I love.

Gross. The word floats through my consciousness like a passing cloud. Acknowledged. Dismissed.

Every body that falls at my feet or by my hand triggers this same response. A surge of power over the absolute finality of things. Proof that I can end existence itself. It's not something I chose. Not something I can control.

Derek. Volkov. The tech billionaire. The boarding school headmistress. The missionary.

I came after every single one.

And I'm not going to stop.

Not for morality. Not for appearances. Not even for her, my perfect, filthy, dark, depraved Scarletta.

Because this is who I am. What I am. The monster she wrote forty-seven stories about without knowing she was describing someone real.

I pull my hand out of my pants, pop the button on my jeans, drag the zipper down, and release myself so she can watch properly.

"This is what it does to me," I say. My voice soft. Soothing. "Killing. It makes me hard. And looking at you right now... all I'm thinking about is... *fucking you.*"

She looks down at herself. Really seeing it for the first time —the spray of blood across her body, the heavier splatter across her chest, the way it's soaked into the fabric of her shirt. Her hands tremble as they reach for the hem, and then she's ripping the shirt over her head in one jerky motion. Underneath, she's wearing a coral-colored sports bra, bright and incongruous against the carnage. Clean.

Then she's bending forward, hooking her thumbs into the waistband of her workout leggings, peeling them down her thighs. The fabric clings to her legs as she works it lower, revealing pale flesh beneath. Unmarked. Untouched by Ryan's blood. She kicks the leggings away, and they land in a crumpled heap next to her discarded shirt.

She straightens, and immediately her arms come up to cross over her chest. Like she's trying to cover herself. To hide. Her shoulders curl inward, making herself smaller, and she stands there in just her bra and panties—looking at me with eyes that are too wide, too bright.

She looks terrified.

I nearly come just thinking that word.

Terrified.

Not of me, though. That's the beautiful part. Not of the man standing three feet away with his cock in his hand, hard from watching her kill. Not of what I might do to her, or what I've already done.

She's terrified of the consequences for what *she* just did.

The balancing of *her* scales. The reckoning she thinks is coming.

I walk over to her slowly, deliberately, my hand still wrapped around my cock because I'm not hiding this from her anymore. When I reach her, I take her wrists—gently, carefully—and pull her arms out, away from her body, letting my cock bob, hard and erect, between us.

She resists for half a second, a tiny whimper catching in her throat, but then she lets me. Lets me hold her arms out to her sides so I can see all of her.

"You balanced him," I tell her. "You delivered justice. Real justice. For Posie. For dozens of others, Scarletta. All those girls whose names we'll never know. You saved dozens more who would've come after them if he'd lived another year, another five, another ten."

"I didn't even decide, Caleb. It just—. I just saw his eyes and I knew, ya know? I knew he was gonna—"

"Shhh," I say, putting a finger against her lip. The blood is still wet. I drag my finger through it, smearing it. Painting her face with it.

She lets me. Not even a flinch. She stares into my eyes like I'm her God. I place my hand on her cheek, look lovingly down at her. I let my thumb trace along her jawline, feeling the tacky warmth of blood there. I can practically hear her heart beating.

"Is your pussy wet?" I ask, my voice dropping. "*Please,* Scarletta. I need to know. Did it make you wet?"

Her mouth falls open. She begins to say something. Stops. Just… stares at me.

I cup her whole face with my hands now. I press my cock into her stomach. My sickness poking in to her. "You can answer honestly. Even if it's no. You can tell me. And if it is no, then… then we'll clean up and I'll take you home. Don't worry about him. I'll take care of him too. You don't have to worry about anything."

I let out a breath. Blink. Swallow.

"But if it's yes, Scarletta. Then… then I would like to fuck you right now. Right here. With his blood all over you. With his destroyed body at our feet. Because this… this isn't my *sickness*. This is my *dream*."

Her eyes search mine. She takes a breath. Holds it. Lets it out with her words. "Why… why don't you check for yourself."

I almost come. Right there. With nothing but her request to spur it. But I hold it in because finally—*finally*—it's happening.

I've found someone.

Someone just like me.

Someone not only willing to balance the scales, but to take payment in a way that breaks all the rules.

Just like her story.

I slide my hand down her stomach. Across the waistband of her panties. And then inside.

Fuck.

She's drenched.

Not wet. Not aroused. *Drenched.* Her pussy is soaked, slick heat coating my fingers the instant I touch her. I have to close my eyes. Have to force myself to breathe through my nose, slow and controlled, because my cock is already twitching and I'm dangerously close to losing it right here with nothing but my hand in her underwear.

She killed a man. She pulled the trigger and watched him die. And her pussy is dripping for it.

I open my eyes and find her watching me. Waiting. Her lips parted, chest heaving, blood drying on her face in dark streaks.

"Good girl," I whisper.

She moans.

The sound breaks something in me. I push two fingers inside her, curling them, and she gasps, her hips bucking forward to meet my hand. She's so wet I can hear it—the obscene squelch of her pussy clenching around my fingers as I fuck her with them.

"You're just like me," I tell her. "You've always been just like me."

"Caleb—" Her voice cracks.

I pull my hand out of her panties and bring my fingers to my mouth. Her taste explodes across my tongue—salt, and musk, and something darker underneath. Something that tastes like adrenaline and fear and the blood-bright edge of death.

I drop to my knees.

The concrete is cold and hard, and Ryan's blood is spreading toward us in a slow creep, and I don't care. I hook my fingers into the waistband of her panties and drag them down her thighs. She steps out of them, and then she's bare from the waist down, standing in nothing but her coral sports bra with a dead man three feet away.

I spread her pussy lips apart with my fingertips and press my tongue into her sick arousal.

She cries out, her hands flying to my head, fingers tangling in my hair. I lick into her, tasting that same darkness, that same violence. My tongue finds her clit and I suck it between my lips, and she makes a sound that's almost a scream.

I eat her like I'm starving. Like she's the only thing that's ever mattered. My tongue works her clit while my fingers push back inside, two and then three, stretching her open. She's grinding against my face now, fucking my mouth, and I can feel her thighs trembling against my cheeks.

"Caleb—Caleb, I'm going to—"

I pull back.

She whimpers, desperate and broken, and I stand up and take her by the hair. I pull her head back so she's looking up at me, and then I guide her down. She goes willingly, sinking to her knees on the blood-spattered concrete, and when I press my cock against her lips she opens her mouth without being told.

I push inside.

Her mouth is hot, and wet, and perfect. I slide deeper, feeling her throat flutter around me, and she gags but doesn't pull away. I hold her there, my cock buried in her throat, and I look down at the blood smeared across her forehead, her cheeks, her chin.

She's the spitting image of the tattoo on my sternum. The one crafted by Posie Little herself. The girl who just got justice.

"Take my cock," I tell Scarletta. "Take all of it."

She does.

I fuck her mouth with slow, deliberate strokes, watching her eyes water, watching drool and blood mix on her chin. She's making desperate little sounds around my cock, and her hand has slipped between her own thighs, fingers working her clit while I use her throat.

I pull out before I come. I'm not finished with her yet.

I haul her up by her hair and spin her around, bending her over a hay bale. Her ass is perfect—round and pale, presented for me. I kick her legs apart and line myself up with her entrance.

I slam inside.

She screams. Not in pain—in relief. In finally getting what she needs. I fuck her hard and deep, my hips slapping against her ass, one hand fisted in her hair and the other wrapped around her throat. She's so wet I can hear it, can feel her pussy gripping me like she never wants to let go.

"You killed him," I growl in her ear. "You pulled the trigger and his blood is all over you and your pussy is soaking my cock."

"Yes," she gasps. "Yes, yes, *yes*—"

I reach around and find her clit. She's so swollen, so sensitive, and when I circle it with two fingers she shatters. Her pussy clamps down on me, milking my cock, and I follow her over the edge with a groan that tears out of my chest.

I come inside her.

I fill her with it, pulse after pulse, and she takes every drop while Ryan's blood dries on both of us.

When it's over, I stay buried inside her, my forehead pressed against her shoulder, both of us breathing hard.

The barn smells like sex, and death, and blood.

And for the first time in my life, I don't feel alone.

For the first time in my life, I feel... *balanced*.

CHAPTER 17
SCARLETTA

EPILOGUE

Sometimes it's really not about the journey.

Sometimes… it really *is* the arrival.

That's how I felt that day I killed Ryan.

Like I arrived somewhere after all that struggle.

All those grinding years of depression that felt like drowning in slow motion.

All the Lucky Charms eaten straight from the box at three in the morning.

All the blanket forts constructed out of fear of being seen.

All the stories with weird monster sex, and submission sex, and every other permutation of darkness I could dream up.

Prophetic and fantasy all wrapped into one sick existence.

My life before killing Ryan was the maze.

Something to be survived.

Life after was… my Helix.

My Caleb.

The monster I could live with.

Who will protect me from the literal darkness I swim in.

Sometimes I catch myself waiting for the other shoe to drop.

Old habit. Hard to kill.

I'll be standing in some gilded ballroom in Monaco, or Singapore, or wherever Caleb's latest charity gala happens to be, wearing a dress that blows my mind when I walk by a mirror, and my brain will whisper: *You don't belong here. They're going to figure it out. Someone's going to tap you on the shoulder and tell you there's been a mistake.*

But nobody ever does.

Caleb watches me across the room during these events. I always know exactly where he is. Some primal GPS in my nervous system that never stops tracking him. He'll be talking to a hedge fund manager, or a tech billionaire, or whoever needs schmoozing, but his eyes find mine every few minutes.

Checking.

Claiming.

Mine.

I used to think that kind of possessiveness would feel suffocating.

Turns out it feels like oxygen.

My laptop comes everywhere now.

Caleb bought me a custom case—hand-stitched Italian leather with my initials embossed in gold. Ridiculous. Obscene. I love it.

I wrote three chapters of my new novel on a private jet somewhere over the Atlantic. Another two in a hotel suite overlooking the Eiffel Tower while Caleb was in meetings. Half a scene in the back of a limousine in Dubai because inspiration struck and I've learned to stop fighting it.

The words come easier now.

Not because my life is easier—it's actually more complicated than ever, filled with schedules, and obligations, and the exhausting performance of being Caleb MacLeay's partner in public—but because I'm not drowning anymore. I'm not writing to survive. I'm writing because I *want* to.

Because I finally have something worth saying.

I published my first novel on Christmas Day.

One year exactly from when Caleb drugged me and left me in my cleaned apartment with an SD card full of footage that should have destroyed me.

Poetic, right?

The book was called *The Watcher*—the same novel I'd been writing for him in those seven weeks after Christmas, back when I thought I was done with him forever. I changed the names. Added some plot. Cleaned up the prose. But it was us. Our story. Every dark, twisted, blood-soaked moment of it.

Caleb read the final draft before I uploaded it. I watched his face the whole time, terrified he'd be angry about me exposing our dynamic, even fictionalized.

He finished the last page, closed my laptop, and fucked me against the wall of his office until I couldn't remember my own name.

Then he told me to publish it.

So I did.

The one-star reviews came fast.

"Disgusting."

"This author needs therapy, not a publishing deal."

"I couldn't finish this. The 'hero' is literally a murderer. How is this romance?"

"Reported for glorifying abuse."

I read them all. Every single one. Caleb found me at two in the morning, curled up in bed with my laptop, laughing so hard tears streamed down my face.

"They hate it," I told him. "They *really* hate it."

"Let them," he said. "They don't deserve your brilliant mind."

My DarkDesires followers—the twelve thousand people who'd been asking where ScarletSins went for a whole year—found the book within hours.

'Someone' told them.

Who could that of been?

I'm looking at you, Masked Man.

The forum exploded. Then TikTok exploded. Then everything exploded.

BookTok creators posted videos defending *The Watcher* with the kind of unhinged passion usually reserved for religious cults.

They made edits set to dramatic music. They wrote essays analyzing the psychological complexity. They posted photos of the text with captions like, "He's a 10 but he fucked her so hard, she blacked out." (Which is kind of a selling point if you ask me.)

Rom Com authors said I was sick.

An unofficial Goodreads poll named me the "Author most likely to need medication".

That 'famous' traditional editor called me a PR disaster on her blog.

I call it seventy-five thousand copies sold in six weeks.

Caleb told me the New York Times bestseller list is curated, not real. That publishers pay for placement. That the whole system is rigged toward certain types of books written by certain types of people, and dark romance erotica written by a nobody from Idaho was never going to make that cut regardless of sales.

I believed him because it made the rejection sting less.

Also because he showed me the receipts.

But here's the thing: I don't need their validation anymore.

The Smut Readers Sacramento Book Signing invited me as a featured author. Me. Scarletta Desmond. ScarletSins. The girl who couldn't function in the real world, who hid in blanket forts, and ate Lucky Charms for dinner, and wrote filthy stories about being owned because she was too broken to ask for love in any normal way.

They want me to sign books and talk on panels and meet the readers who understand my darkness.

And I'm going to go.

With Caleb.

As my trophy husband.

We're getting married in ten days.

Valentine's Day.

One year exactly from when I walked into a maze of my own making and came out the other side holding a shotgun and a kill count.

One year from when I finally stopped running from the monster I craved and let him catch me.

The dress is obscene—white silk that clings to every curve, a slit up to my hip, a neckline that would make my mother weep.

The ceremony will be small. Private. Just us and a few people from his world who know what he really does and don't flinch.

No family on my side. Obviously.

But I have my DarkDesires followers sending virtual congratulations. I have my laptop with three more novels outlined. I have a man who sees every ugly, shameful, blood-soaked corner of my psyche and calls it beautiful.

I have a future.

Sometimes I think about the girl I was a year ago.

Drowning in her own patterns. Watching herself drown. Writing stories about being saved because she didn't believe it could happen in real life.

She was right, in a way.

This isn't being saved.

This is being *claimed*.

By someone just as broken. Just as dark. Just as hungry for the things nice people pretend don't exist.

I found my Helix.

My monster.

My Caleb.

We walk the darkness together now.

And yes, it's just as fucked-up as it sounds.

But it's honest.

And it's real.

And it's... *ours*.

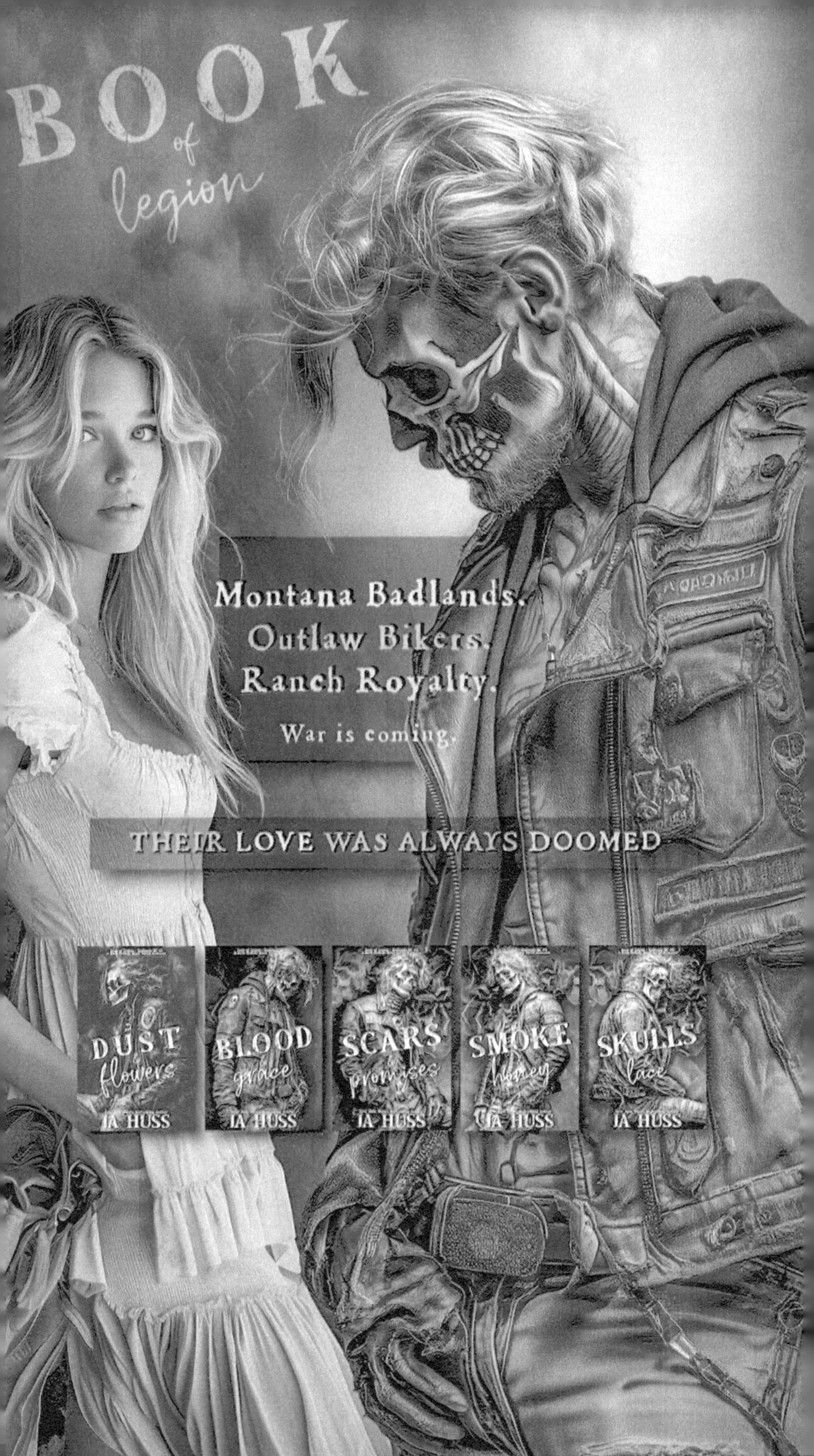

BOOK of legion
Montana Badlands.
Outlaw Bikers.
Ranch Royalty.
War is coming.
THEIR LOVE WAS ALWAYS DOOMED
DUST flowers
JA HUSS
BLOOD grace
JA HUSS
SCARS promises
JA HUSS
SMOKE honey
JA HUSS
SKULLS lace
JA HUSS

BOOK OF LEGION

Dust and Flowers
A Dark Outlaw Biker Serial Romance
Book of Legion – Badlands MC #1
By JA Huss

Savannah Ashby has been photographed 70,000 times—every smile, every outfit, every moment of her perfect ranch heiress life has been documented on social media by her dead mother's cameras.

Legion Kane came out of Whitefall Prison with nothin' but an expired driver's license, $27 in his wallet, and a name that means biblical demon possession.

She wears another man's three-carat diamond.

He wears a fresh MC brand burned into his chest.

This star-crossed couple have been meeting in secret at an abandoned silo since they were kids.

Now her family wants him dead, his MC wants him loyal, and the only thing that matters is what happens when she meets him at midnight, whisperin' his name like a prayer.

Montana badlands.
Outlaw bikers.
Ranch royalty.

War is coming.

DUST AND FLOWERS

Their secret just became everyone's problem.

VIBES…

🏍️💏🔥 Outlaw Biker Romance
💸🖤🔧 Rich Girl / Poor Boy
💏🔒🖤 Property Of
🖤🔪⚔️ Morally Gray / Anti-Hero MMC
🔥👁️💏 Obsessed / Possessive MMC
🚫🖤🔪 Forbidden Love
🙌💍🖤 Only Her
🖤⚔️🔥 Only Him
🤍🏠 Childhood Sweethearts
⚔️🔪💀 Touch Her and Die
🔥🌶️😳 Primal Spice
😇🔒🖤 Secret Relationship

END OF BOOK SHIT

Welcome to the End of Book Shit. This is the part of the book where I get to say anything I want about the book you just read. It's never edited, so please excuse any typos.

———

All right. Dead Daze. What a ride.

I really enjoyed writing this book. It was fun. At no point did I ever wake up and say, ah, man. I gotta write that today. Nope. And yeah, I get it—it's not that deep. It's pretty surface-level, actually. But this is the story of Scarletta's fucking arrival and I dug it.

The part where she realizes that Helix is real and she loves him—that was my full-circle moment in this series. Once again, I didn't mean to set it up that way, the muse just showed up, like it always does, and filled in the gaps I left for it. Because the parallel to *Call of the Labyrinth* is everything IMO.

In that story, Lyra runs through a maze thinking there's a portal home at the center, gets captured and violated three times by monsters, and when she finally reaches the end—guess what? No portal.

Just Helix waiting.

The "escape" was always a lie. Her choice was never freedom versus captivity—it was which monster she'd submit to.

Helix wasn't the good guy. He was just *her* guy. The lesser evil who'd protect her from worse evils.

That's Scarletta's entire arc in Dead Daze.

She spends six months trying to escape Caleb by dating normal men, getting a glow-up in Vegas, and pretending she's moved on.

Ryan seems like the safe choice—yeah, he's got a filming kink and some weird equipment, but that's manageable vanilla compared to Caleb's "I get hard torturing people to death" energy.

Ryan's her portal home to normalcy.

Except there is no portal.

There never was.

Ryan was going to film her murder for a snuff site. The "safe" option was literally going to kill her.

And suddenly Caleb—the stalker who hacked her apartment, the killer who came on corpses, the obsessive who tattooed her face on his body before they met is her soul mate.

Her Helix. He's the monster who *protects* her from monsters.

When Scarletta shoots Ryan, she's not choosing Caleb over Ryan. She's choosing to stop running from what she actually is.

She's Lyra reaching the center of the maze and realizing she was never going home.

We have arrival.

They're not broken people trying to fix each other. They're broken people who fit together perfectly *because* of how they're broken.

I feel like this epilogue is truly earned in a way that matters greatly.

What a difference a year makes.

We've all experienced this. We've all had that 'one year' when life flipped. Sometimes it's a terrible flip. But every once in a while, it's a miracle.

Scarletta's ending feels like a miracle she earned.

One year later, she's published *The Watcher*, she's marrying Caleb on Valentine's Day, she's attending book signings with twelve thousand DarkDesires followers backing her. She's not hiding behind ScarletSins anymore. She's Scarletta Desmond, and she writes fucked-up rape fantasies about being stalked by killers because that's… what she likes to write.

She's not looking for readers. She doesn't care about reviews, or feelings, or opinions.

This.

Is what.

She writes.

As far as the EOBS for the series as a whole—we've followed two people who spent their entire lives convinced they were irredeemably broken find love.

That's pretty much it.

Scarletta realizes that her darkest fantasy (being hunted, captured, violated, and discovering the escape was a lie) is a blueprint for her actual psychology.

This is how her brain works.

She doesn't write these pitch-black scenes because she's damaged. She writes them because her sexuality is wired around fear, surrender, and being claimed by someone who sees through all her walls.

The maze in her story isn't metaphor.

It's a diagnosis.

Triple X-Mas is her first capture. Willing Chaff is her second (interrupted by real violence). Dead Daze is her third and final—where she stops fighting and accepts this is who she is.

Just like Lyra's three captures in the Labyrinth.

Except Scarletta's ending is better because she *chooses* Caleb with full knowledge. She shoots Ryan. She fucks Caleb next to the body. She publishes the book about their relationship. She marries him. That's agency Lyra never got.

Caleb's journey is... honestly, I don't think he grows. I think he just *arrives* too.

Caleb shows up in Chapter 1 already fully formed. He's a billionaire who runs a vigilante murder organization called The Scales. He gets hard from torturing predators to death. He's obsessed with a woman he's been stalking for six months. He's tattooed her face on his body from *years before meeting her.*

He's not on a redemption arc.

He's not learning to be better.

He's Helix, and Helix doesn't change.

Helix just draws Lyra *to him.*

What Caleb does is *fall in love,* and that's different from growth. He starts the series wanting to own Scarletta. He ends it still wanting to own her, but now he also wants her *happy.* He wants her writing. He wants her confident. He wants her at galas with him, in his bed, publishing books, attending signings. The possessiveness doesn't go away—it just expands to include her personhood.

His MO is literally called The Scales. Balance. Justice. He's looking for equilibrium, and Scarletta is his counterweight.

She's the only person who can watch his true, fucked-up self and not run away.

She's the only person who makes him feel not alone.

That's not character development. That's *finding your match.*

The series isn't about broken people healing. It's about broken people finding someone whose damage fits their damage perfectly.

It's about the relief of being seen completely—the stalking, the murder, the rape fantasies, the voyeurism, the violence—and having someone say, "Yeah, me too."

The romance isn't "love conquers all." It's "love is finding someone equally monstrous."

And that's honestly—for me, anyway—far more interesting than a redemption arc.

The reason this series works (for me, what you think is up to you) is because it's honest about desire.

Most dark romance tries to soften the edges—"he's only violent because trauma," "she only likes it because she's healing," whatever.

This series is a big 'ol "Fuck that".

They're like this because that's who they are.

Scarletta gets off on fear.

Caleb gets off on control and violence.

They're not going to therapy.

They're getting married and writing books about it.

That's arrival at the center of the maze.

Welcome home.

Thank you for reading, thank you for reviewing, and I'll see you in the next book!

Julie

JA Huss

January 26, 2026

P.S. - If you'd like more Scarletta and Caleb, let me know in your reviews. I'd love to write more 'Playroom' scenes! :)

ABOUT THE AUTHOR

JA Huss is a scientist, New York Times and USA Today bestselling author. Her self-published romantasy Sparktopia was named an Audible Editors' Best of the Year selection in 2024, and several of her audiobooks have been nominated for the Audie and SOVA Awards. A 2019 RITA finalist, Huss has had five books optioned for film and television and co-wrote a television pilot for MGM with actor and screenwriter Jonathan McClain.